CIRCLE OF FIRE

THE WITCH'S PROGRESS
BOOK TWO

LEAH R CUTTER

KNOTTED ROAD PRESS

Reviews
It's true. Reviews help me sell more books. If you've enjoyed this story, please consider leaving a review of it on your favorite site.

Come someplace new…
Are you a traveler? Do you enjoy exploring strange new worlds, new cultures, new people?

Journey into the various lands envisioned by Leah R Cutter.

Sign up for my newsletter and I'll start you on your travels with a free copy of my book, *The Island Sampler*.

http://www.LeahCutter.com/newsletter/

Buy More!
Did you know that you can buy directly from the Knotted Road Press website?

https://www.knottedroadpress.com/shop/

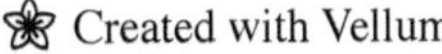 Created with Vellum

THE CIRCLES OF WITCHCRAFT

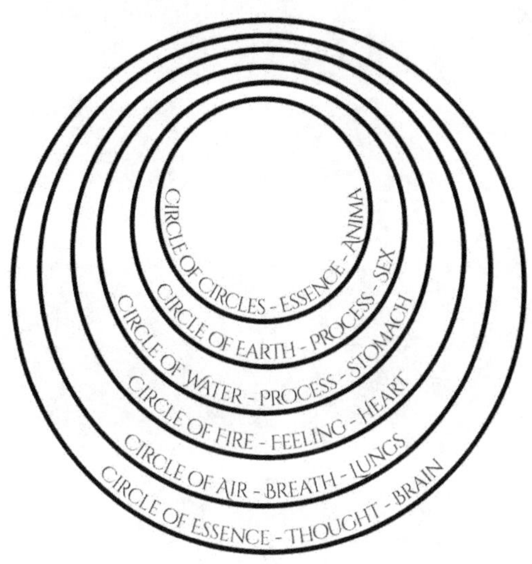

ALSO BY LEAH R CUTTER

Urban/Contemporary Fantasy Series

The Witch's Progress

Circle of Air

Circle of Fire

Circle of Water

Circle of Earth

The Shadow Wars Trilogy

The Raven and the Dancing Tiger

The Guardian Hound

War Among the Crocodiles

The Cassie Stories

Poisoned Pearls

Tainted Waters

Spoiled Harvest

Bloodied Ice

Seattle Trolls

The Changeling Troll

The Princess Troll

The Fairy-Bridge Troll

The Troll-Demon War

The Troll-Human War

The Troll-Troll War

The Clockwork Fairy Kingdom

The Clockwork Fairy Kingdom

The Maker, the Teacher, and the Monster

The Dwarven Wars

The Chronicles of Franklin

Franklin Versus The Popcorn Thief

Franklin Versus The Soul Thief

Franklin Versus The Child Thief

Epic Fantasy Series

The Fallen Elves

Ruins of the Gods

Stairs of the Gods

Cities of the Gods

Graves of the Gods

Houses of the Dead

Houses Divided

Houses Fallen

Houses Reborn

Forgotten Gods

A Wind Blown Torment

A Stone Strewn Clash

A Sea Washed Victory

The Tanesh Empire Trilogy

The Glass Magician

The Desert Heart

The Ghost Dog

Science Fiction

The Long Run

Project Nemesis

Project Nyx

Project Tisiphone

Project Persephone

War of the Allied Worlds

The Labors of Darius Linard

Huli Intergalactic: Science/Space Fantasy

Origins

The Strawberry Girl

Mysteries

The Purloined Letter Opener

The Tell Tale Heart Pin

Dancer in Darkness

Trophy Hunters

The Alvin Goodfellow Case Files

The Rabbit Mysteries

The Shredded Veil Mysteries

Mystery, Crime, and Mayhem

CHAPTER 1

While I was at the headwaters for the mighty Willamette, I sacrificed an entire coven of witches to the river god Mulinohana, to ensure His forbearance when sending his flood waters toward the newly born city of Portland. Now that I have returned to the city, I need to renew the vows of the river god, to mark each and every one of the mighty bridges as His so that He might spare them. However, that means finding more witches. I need at least one for each bridge now being built or rebuilt, to lash a witch's heart to the footing and bind her there. The Hawthorn bridge is currently being reconstructed, with the project to be finished by 1901. I need to go hunting.

Wilson Evermore, Civil Engineer and Chief Magician,
1900

"Stop! Stay still!"

Tara froze. What on earth?

Okay, so maybe she was harvesting rose hips in public. But it wasn't as though she was doing anything illegal. She was in a public park. This was public property.

The day was sunny and unusually warm for Portland, particularly given that it was the middle of September. Still, it seemed the perfect time to harvest. Bright orange, red, and even purple rose hips peeked out from the green leaves and thorns of the *Rosa Rugosa* plants that ran through the center of the park. Some of the flowers had been confused by the hot summer, and were still blooming. As Tara had walked along the gravel path, their heady scent had followed her.

Tara started to turn around to address the speaker, to protest her innocence.

"Are you daft? Didn't you hear me? Stay still!"

Tara froze again, puzzled. The voice addressing her was female, and now that she thought about it, had a very slight British accent to it.

"Why?" Tara finally asked.

"There's wasps right in front of you!"

Tara looked closer at the roses nearest her. Sure enough, yellow jackets buzzed not two inches from her bare fingers.

As that type of wasp tended to be attracted by movement, and was also aggressive, the other woman's advice finally made sense.

However, Tara was also a powerful witch. She'd assembled a sachet for herself that morning to protect her from the thorns of the roses, as well as any insects. She'd combined lemon balm and chamomile to soothe and calm, borage and angelica for protection, as well as caraway, cloves, and rosemary for general good luck. The pouch itself was made out of plain cotton that Tara had first "fixed" with salt and magic (so the color wouldn't just wash out the first time she got the cloth wet), then dyed a gentle pink using rose petals.

The wasps wouldn't bother her. They hadn't even noticed her standing there.

Still, it wouldn't do for her to ignore this woman's advice. Most people knew nothing about magic. Tara wasn't about to show off her talent.

Instead, she stayed frozen a few more moments, as if she was making certain that the wasps weren't bothered by her. Then she slowly began to back away, stepping out of the rose bushes and onto the gravel path behind her. Only then did Tara turn to the woman who'd "saved" her.

A short young woman stood on the path. She had a mop of bright red curls on the top of her head, though it was shaved along the sides, giving her a cool, edgy look. Geometric tattoos—connected triangles and octagons—ran from behind her ears down her neck, as if streams of art just flowed naturally from her. A gold loop pierced her left nostril, and an entire row of rings ran up the edges of both of her ears, like modern armor, as well as bars pierced through her inner lobes.

She looked to be about Tara's age, in her mid-thirties. Freckles covered her pert nose and across her rounded cheeks, making her appear younger, while her green eyes held a depth of living. Her broad smile promised mischief.

She wore a baggy, long-sleeved, green-and-white striped shirt, jeans, and had a flowered sunhat that she'd pushed back from her face, hanging by a cord around her neck.

Tara pushed her own sunhat off her head so she could see the other woman better. Tara was dressed in a T-shirt, shorts, and sandals—then again, her coloring was darker than the other woman's. She would tan in the sun, whereas she was certain the redhead in front of her would fry to a crisp if she wasn't completely covered. Tara wore her own brown hair tied back in a tight ponytail, as usual. At five foot ten, she felt as though she towered over the other woman, who was five feet tall, at the most.

"Thank you," Tara said, smiling at the woman.

Then she noticed that the other woman held equipment very similar to her own: a pair of clippers in one hand and a cloth bag in the other.

"Oh! Were you harvesting as well?" Tara asked, holding up her own bag of rose hips.

The other woman nodded. "Seems a waste not to." The accent she had was very slight. How long had she been in the States? "Me Gran couldn't abide a waste."

"I'm just cheap," Tara said with a shrug. "Much less expensive for me to just harvest what's here. My name's Tara, by the way."

"Ginny," the other woman replied. She peered at Tara for a moment. "How will you process them?"

A deep rift existed between people who gathered

rose hips, depending on the method used to process them, like a religious schism. Tara had witnessed two witches almost coming to blows over it at the shop.

"For tea, I'll process them the modern way, first drying them in a food dehydrator, then using a food processor to break them apart, and a sieve to separate out the hairs," Tara admitted. "For everything else, I'll do it the old fashioned way, slicing the rose hips and scooping out the insides before I dry them. How about you?"

Ginny gave her a big grin, then leaned closer, as if sharing a secret. "Much the same," she said. "Though me Gran would have a fit if she ever found out I'd been using those newfangled modern tools."

"I hear you," Tara said. "The—the woman who first taught me about plants would also throw a fit if she found out I was using, gasp, *machines*."

Ginny snorted at her. "Aye," she said. "So I've been coming up the path this way," she said, pointing behind her.

"And I've been working the other direction," Tara said. Between the pair of them, they'd just about covered one side of the path, starting at the ends and working toward the middle. "Should we switch to the other side?"

Just across the gravel path ran another long bed of roses. It wasn't as long or as deep as the first side, but Tara had been planning on harvesting on that side as well.

"Sure," Ginny said agreeably. "I haven't been in the

city for long. Wasn't sure if this kind of thing was proper."

"I've been here since I finished college, coming up on fifteen years, now," Tara said. "No one's ever bothered me, though I've had lots of people curious about what I was doing. Where were you before this?"

"Ach, here and there," Ginny said. "Was born in Wales. Was there until me Gran died, ten years gone this fall." She was silent a moment, taking a deep breath, obviously still in mourning for her gram.

"I'm sorry for your loss," Tara said sincerely.

Ginny shrugged as she turned toward the rose bushes. "It pushed me outta the nest. Got me across the pond."

"Do you like it here?" Tara asked.

Again, the non-committal shrug as Ginny clipped a cherry-tomato-red rose hip from the bush in front of her. She trimmed both ends off before she dropped the hip into her bag. "Well enough. Still trying to find my way, you know?"

"I hear you," Tara said. Her own life had been turned completely upside down that summer. Though it had been no more than three months ago, it seemed like several lifetimes at this point. She no longer had a coven of witches to call her own. She was staying with her best friend Kyle for the time being, in his spare bedroom, but she needed to find someplace else and soon.

Tara still occasionally picked up shifts at *Ye Olde Magick Shoppe* in downtown Portland. However, even that remnant of her old life would dry up soon. The owner, Patricia, had finally found a permanent replacement for her. Not that Tara had wanted to leave, but none of the regular witches wanted to deal with her, afraid that she'd cause them bad luck. She had to find a job. Her savings would run out in a month's time. However, she felt stuck, unable to move forward, and she wasn't certain why.

Tara and Ginny worked together for a few moments in silence, each absorbed in selecting the perfect rose hips. Due to the hot summer, the hips had frequently gone past ripe and straight to withered. Tara would find one that looked perfect on top, only to lift it up and find that it was soft and squishy underneath. She settled for hips that were less ripe and more firm in an effort to fill up her bag, though they wouldn't be as flavorful as the hips that were fully ripe.

"Will you be making oil from these?" Tara asked as she clipped a vibrant purple hip. The color didn't affect the taste, but Tara still liked the purple ones the best.

"Aye," Ginny replied. "And some balms. I have a friend who lets me share her booth sometimes, down in the Saturday Market. And you?"

"I'll make tea as well as oil," Tara said. "Mainly, though, I hope to sell the processed rose hips. You know *Ye Olde Magick Shoppe* downtown?"

Ginny nodded slowly. "I do," she said. She looked over at Tara quizzically. "You think they'll take some of these for their supplies? In that fancy back room of theirs?"

Tara perked up. While the front of the Magick Shoppe was a tourist destination, complete with wands, crystals, and pyramids of energy that held no magic at all, the back room carried real supplies for the local witches and other beings of power. The room was hidden in plain sight. Most of the tourists didn't even realize it was there. The only people who even noticed it were beings who had magic, whether they knew it or not.

Ginny asking about the back room meant that not only had she seen it, she had power.

"They might take some of your processed hips," Tara said. "I work there." Patricia had told Tara that she'd buy any hips that Tara was willing to sell, primarily because Patricia would be able to charge a premium for them, as they'd been collected and processed by a witch.

"Oh!" Ginny said. She took a hasty step back and away. "You're one of them! A schooled witch. Sorry to be a bother to ye."

With that, Ginny took off down the path in haste.

"Wait!" Tara called after her, but the girl had disappeared. Had she used some sort of illusion to hide her from seeking eyes? She'd called it up quickly if she had.

What had spooked her? Had she had a run in with some of the other witches in Portland? And what did she mean by a "schooled" witch?

Tara shook her head. Yes, she might be considered a "schooled witch" by some. As part of her training in the coven, she'd had to learn not only the Latin names of the herbs she used, where they grew and how to cultivate them, as well as the traditional medicinal, culinary, and utilitarian properties of each, she then had to layer on the actual magical potions that the plants were used in. Often the traditional magic assigned to a plant was similar to the real magical power, but sometimes it wasn't.

However, since Tara had left her coven (or been kicked out for bringing *bad luck*, depending on how you looked at it) she'd stopped learning the traditional way, or at least cramming as much as she could into her head when she had spare time. Instead, she was starting to figure out her own approach to magic, as well as the herbs and plants she used.

Kyle had called her a *hedgewitch*, one that worked with the natural elements of things instead of following the strict traditions.

Tara was still trying to find her path, just as she was still trying to get her feet back under her from the blows of the summer.

But what did that make Ginny? Was she also a hedgewitch? Or just an untrained woman with power?

Tara considered for a moment. She wasn't content with just letting Ginny be. There was something there, some sort of connection that she'd had with Tara.

It was only Thursday. That weekend, Tara was going to the Saturday market, and see if she could find Ginny again.

TARA WAS ELBOWS DEEP IN ROSE HIPS, AS IT WERE, when Kyle came home that evening from his office job.

He clerked for the federal court downtown, having decided early in his career that he didn't want to work as a lawyer on his own, though he had a degree in law. He always said he worked better behind the scenes, influencing a judge's opinions, rather than having to do all the case work himself.

Kyle always dressed the part of a powerful lawyer for work. That day he wore an expensive light-gray suit that looked good against his black skin, a brilliant white shirt, and a red power tie. Expensive, black-leather Italian shoes completed the outfit. His bald head just added to his gravitas, as did his physique, all the muscles he worked hard to keep up at the gym. He was also taller than Tara, six foot three, as well as older, as they'd just celebrated his forty-fifth birthday.

Though Kyle looked impressive and kept a serious demeanor, Tara counted herself privileged to know what a goof Kyle could be. They still had Friday night movie nights together, laughing themselves silly at bad seventies movies.

They'd been living together for two and a half months now, long enough for Tara to know Kyle's routine. He merely nodded at her as he emptied his pockets of his wallet, phone, loose change, and so on. Then he went directly to his bedroom, already stripping.

Tara had seen more of Kyle's body than friends normally shared. Then again, he was gay, and she had the wrong equipment.

She kept her head down, refocusing on the rose hips in front of her. She'd already set one large batch to drying, the hips that she'd keep for herself to make tea and sachets from. The rest, as she'd told Ginny before the woman ran off, she was processing by hand.

It was a long, fiddly business, slicing the hips apart and scooping out the insides by hand. She was doing them in batches, slicing a large amount, then scraping the insides out, then slicing another large amount. The hips themselves were slimy, and despite how Tara had tried to pick only the brightest, ripest hips, the seeds on the inside would stick and she'd end up scraping away too much of the skin.

She hadn't taken all of the hips from the park that were ripe. She'd just gone down "her" side of the row of roses, from the middle to the end, leaving the other half for Ginny if she decided to go back.

Tara had found herself thinking about Ginny off and on all afternoon. It wasn't sexual, Tara wasn't attracted to the girl. (Tara tended to be heterosexual, but she was open minded. It was Portland, after all.) It was more like meeting a long-lost friend. If the Saturday market had been open that afternoon, Tara would have already gone to it, looking for Ginny.

Once Tara heard the shower get turned off, she started packing up her mess, making room for Kyle in the kitchen. Part of Kyle's routine after work included first showering off the day, then meditating for a while before he came out to the kitchen and cooked dinner.

Tara had tried to cook dinner for them a few times when she'd first moved in, as part of her payment for the free room and board. However, Kyle insisted that he keep up his routine. Cooking was meditative for him. Tara actually understood that, and so always tried to vacate the kitchen and have everything cleaned up by the time he came out.

She needed to find a job. And a place to live. And a coven who would take her.

Though Tara had survived her encounter with the Riprap man, none of the covens in Portland would have anything to do with her. They considered her *bad luck*. That was what had happened in the past for any witch who had at least temporarily escaped the Riprap man. He'd come after not only them, but everyone they knew.

That hadn't happened, at least not as far as Tara knew.

Had the river god killed his faithful servant? Tara had assumed so.

Except that the last few nights, she'd started having nightmares again. Nothing obvious, no. She'd be doing something normal when she'd feel a pressure at her back as if someone was staring at her from across the room, but when she turned around, no one was there. The smell of water had started to follow her everywhere as well, dank and cold.

By the time Kyle came out of his room, Tara had cleaned up her mess, pushing the processed and unprocessed hips into two containers to the side. He gave her a grave smile as he passed her, making a beeline for the kitchen.

"Feeling human again?" Tara asked. He looked good. He wore a green and white shirt that looked inspired by afrofuturism, along with jeans and bare feet.

"I am," Kyle said solemnly. He opened up the refrigerator and paused, thinking. "How about stir fry tonight? We have leftover chicken and plenty of veggies."

That had been one thing that Tara had been able to get Kyle to change. He'd been in the habit of having bread and pasta and just drinking a veggie protein shake instead of eating real vegetables. Now he'd become a master at stir fry, particularly as Tara had slowly added more veggies to their shared fridge/freezer.

"Stir fry sounds great," Tara said. "What can I help with?"

Kyle scowled at the open fridge for a moment, before he slowly pulled out a bok choy. "I'm not even sure what to do with that, that, mutant cabbage thing," he commented.

Tara grinned. "Both the green leaves and the white stems are edible. When it was just me, I'd buy one of these large bok choy, chop it up, then throw half in the freezer for smoothies and half in the fridge for salads."

"Kewl. You could teach a cooking class, you know. Down at the local co-op," Kyle said. He was forever coming up with possible work for her, knowing that she wanted to find a new job.

That actually wasn't a bad idea. "Vegetables you may not know?" Tara said.

The question remained, however, did she just want to string together several one-off gigs? Or did she want to try to get just a single job, and a single, reliable paycheck?

A single job meant a reasonably regular schedule; however, Tara was well aware that she'd probably end up working retail, which meant lots of hours.

Being a permanent freelancer meant she'd constantly be hustling for work on the one hand. It also meant setting her own hours, and larger chunks of time for her magical studies.

She could always go back to being an *au pair* which would include room and board. However, those jobs also meant being at someone's beck and call, much like working retail, for worse pay.

Tara brought herself back to the job at hand, dismantling the large bok choy. She and Kyle worked together in silence for a short while, applying themselves to their separate chopping blocks. Kyle had started on the carrots, chopping those up, and had turned to the cauliflower next.

Tara had learned not to ask Kyle about his day job. He kept a strict separation between it and his home life. It was one of the ways he was, to use his words, "able to stay a nice guy and not turn into an asshole lawyer type."

After a while, Kyle did ask, "How did your day go?"

Tara told Kyle about meeting Ginny, and the feeling that she had about needing to go find the girl, as if they had unfinished business.

Kyle had already started frying the carrots and celery by the time she was finished.

"Witches form covens," he said slowly. "While there are some who work alone, most work together in a group. A tight-knit community."

Tara nodded. She'd had her friend Richard—a research librarian who always needed more work—look up the history of covens. There was an ancient tradition of them, dating back to Egyptian times (though Richard had complained long and bitterly about how much more difficult it was to research anything Egyptian since those stupid teenaged vampire movies had come out).

"I don't think it's in your nature to work alone," Kyle continued.

Tara sighed. "You're right," she said. While she didn't consider herself an extrovert, one of the things she missed most about working in the shop was more interaction with people. Which was why working at retail might turn out to be her best choice.

"We've talked before about you forming your own coven," Kyle said. He splashed some vinegar into the pot, causing the cooking vegetables to sputter. "Do you think Ginny might be part of that?"

Tara blinked, surprised by his suggestion. However, she immediately felt the rightness of his statement. "Wow," she said. "I would never have thought of that. I think you may be right, though."

Kyle nodded. "Your coven won't be traditional," he said with a grin.

He'd said that before. Tara had always just agreed with him. Finally, though, it occurred to her that they might have different ideas about what that meant.

"Tell me more about what you see for a non-traditional coven," Tara said. She was still unwilling to commit to calling it *her* coven. She wasn't a practitioner of the inner circle, and those were generally the only witches to collect a coven to them. Officially, she was only at first level, in the circle of thought. She'd been trying to move into the circle of air when the lead witch of her coven had cheated and Tara had failed the test.

Unofficially, Tara considered herself a witch of the circle of air, because of how close she'd come, as well as how difficult the test had been—much more difficult than the standard tests. Plus, she would have passed the test if the head of her old coven hadn't cheated.

"You're going to have different people in your coven, different from the norm," Kyle said after a moment. "People like Richard."

"What?" Tara asked, outraged. "But he isn't a witch! He's completely mundane!" The librarian was an old boyfriend of hers that she'd had to leave because he'd gotten too inquisitive about her magical side. Turned out he'd made some pretty accurate guesses about her being a witch, though he didn't really understand that she could do magic.

Or did he know? She'd never asked him outright. He was now seeing a lovely girl, Jeannie, who Tara had not only met but approved of. It made things much easier between them.

After a moment, Kyle continued. "True, Richard isn't a witch. He has no magical powers. But he has other powers, powers that you need, like his ability to look up old lore for you, find texts and passages. In a traditional coven, the eldest would keep the sacred books and would have a network for locating relevant information. You will need to build your own."

"Huh," Tara said. She'd never considered that Richard might be part of the coven. He could never be a full member, doing magic properly, but maybe she could make him an honorary one…

"Okay," Tara finally said after thinking it over for a bit. "Who else?"

"Well, me, of course," Kyle said, giving her a sly grin. He'd quit the old coven in protest over how they'd treated Tara. Aaloka, the second in command of the coven, had met with Tara afterwards, but had waffled about leaving. She, at least, had stayed in touch with Tara. They had a weekly coffee date every Friday afternoon.

"Do you need a coven?" Tara asked. Kyle seemed, well, pretty self-contained.

"I do," Kyle said solemnly. "I like the flow of energy that only happens in the circle, the way our prayers slide out into the world."

"Then maybe Ginny, and me," Tara said. "Who else?"

Kyle shrugged. "That's for you to figure out," he said. "Once you put your mind to it, the witches will come."

Tara had no answer for that. It was, however, how things frequently worked, that serendipitous magic.

It was time for her to set her intention and form her own coven. Whatever it might look like.

Tara dreamed that night of fighting the Riprap man again. Only this time, it wasn't just her tied to the footing of the Burnside Bridge, far beneath the water.

Five other figures were tied there as well. Though traditional myths always said that covens were composed of thirteen witches, six or eleven was more accurate. There were six circles, and a coven generally had at least one practitioner of each circle, or possibly two, with only one witch who practiced at the inner most level, the circle of circles, also known as anima, or essence.

In the dream, dark hoods covered the heads of her fellow captives. They struggled as she did with the hard, heavy rope tying them to the bridge. They all stood on the riprap—the boulders piled up at the bottom of the footing for a bridge to protect it from both the water as well as boats.

Tara tried to call out to her fellow witches, to encourage them, but the water carried away her words. The rocks under her bare feet were slimy, and she kept slipping as she struggled.

Though the water's temperature was comfortable, a cold current was snaking its way toward Tara, like a dark serpent. It foretold the coming of the Riprap man, the creature who had tried to sacrifice Tara to the river god earlier that year, just after the summer solstice.

Tara had made a separate deal with the river god, to honor him by scattering rose petals on the equinoxes. In the dream, she realized to her horror that she'd forgotten. The rose petals still filled the pockets of the jacket she wore.

If only she could get her hands free! She might stop the fate slowly rolling toward her if she could just reach the river god again.

But she couldn't free herself.

One by one, her companions all burst their ropes, either through physical strength (was that Kyle?) or through making the rope burn. One had even transformed the rope into a living vine which had then gracefully rolled away from its captive.

None of them tried to save her, though. As soon as they were free, they floated up toward the surface and were gone.

The Riprap man was coming for Tara's soul.

Tara tried calling up her powers, using what she'd learned. Fire fizzled around her. Try as she might, she couldn't direct it. The pattern of scars the fire had left during her last battle, the ones that circled her belly, seemed shrunken and blistered over. Bubbles of air lifted her up, but they weren't strong enough to pull her away from the ropes. The water surrounding her gave her strength. It was growing weaker though, as the dark waters carried by the Riprap man overtook the natural waters of the river. Tara stood on solid rock which wouldn't listen to her: she was more in tune with earth than stone.

In the distance, Tara got a glimpse of the Riprap man. His face was hazy even in the clear water. His torso still appeared to be made out of rocks, like the riprap she stood on. However, he seemed diminished, smaller than she remembered him.

As he drew closer, she could tell that the rocks which composed his body were no longer as well assembled as they'd once been. Before, he'd looked more like a superhero drawing of a rock man. Now, he shambled, the rocks piled up haphazardly. One shoulder stood higher than the other, as if he'd become a hunchback. He also limped now, one leg shorter than the other.

Dark magic swirled around his head, pouring out filth into the river.

The sluggish, oily cloud reached out to Tara, encasing her. She shuddered at the clutching feel of it, how it circled her arms and her chest. Slime that covered her, seeking to pollute her soul.

She had to get her hands free! Had to grab her rose petals. Had to go find her friends, the rest of her coven, even though they'd abandoned her.

Before the dirt and grime swallowed her whole.

At least now her water power helped by trying to keep her skin clean. The battle seemed endless, though. As soon as Tara switched her concentration from her hands to her legs, the filth came pouring back. Itchy welts raised across her bare skin, infected sores filled with pus.

Cold black eyes stared out from the face of the Riprap man, sucking at her like dark whirlpools, willing her soul to rise up out of her body.

"No. Never," Tara said.

Only then did she realize her mistake. By opening her mouth, she gave the filth surrounding her the opportunity to dive straight into her.

The blackness slid down her throat, more bitter than one of Miss Lucy's potions, curling around her tongue and making her gag. She felt the long worms sliding through her stomach, then blooming outward, infecting her limbs, her heart, her lungs.

Tara cried out the one word that she knew might save her.

"DREAM!"

The realization that she was merely dreaming woke her right up.

She sat up, finding herself still in Kyle's spare bedroom. The cold from her nightmare followed her, making her shiver. With a shaking hand she reached over and turned on the light on the end table, banishing the dark shadows.

Books covered the walls, old law books and text books, stiff and formal, not comforting. A chest of drawers made from a dark wood stood at the foot of the bed, matching the bookcases, heavy and masculine. Tara's bright blue suitcases gathered in the corner next to the chest, the only color in the room, the rest of her clothes there. A single window facing west filled much of the adjacent wall, the shade letting too much light seep through.

Tara made herself take a deep breath, then another. She couldn't get warm, though.

What she really wanted to do was to get up and take a shower, both to warm herself up, as well as get herself clean again, really clean. However, that would wake Kyle up, and he had to go to work in the morning. It wouldn't be fair to him.

Instead, Tara pulled her ratty but soft and warm green bathrobe out of the tiny closet that mostly held Kyle's winter suits and wrapped it around her before going out to the kitchen to make herself some tea. Kyle would sleep through that if she was quiet.

She didn't turn on any lights in the two-bedroom condo, the windows of the patio shining with enough light from the city outside. With practiced movements, Tara found her large mug and her electric tea kettle, filling it with just enough water and plugging it in before she opened the cupboard dedicated to her herbs.

Without thinking about it, Tara pulled out lemon balm, peppermint, and chamomile to help calm her down. To that mix, she added some stinging nettle, for cleansing, as well as a pinch of lavender, which would do double duty, both for calming as well as spiritual cleaning. She hesitated, but finally added a pinch of borage as well, for courage.

When her tea had finished steeping, Tara sat down on the cool leather couch facing the sliding glass doors, her hands wrapped around her mug, and thought about her dream.

It had been more than just a nightmare. That much she knew. The dream had the same foretelling quality of the first time she'd dreamed of the Riprap man.

Tara now knew that the Riprap man had survived his battle with the river god. Had he killed Mulinohana? Was that why Tara hadn't been able to call on the river god? Had the Riprap man bound the spirit of the river? Or had the pair of them come to a new agreement?

She had no answers, only more questions. Why was the Riprap man coming for her now? Why hadn't he started his attack the next day?

With a start, Tara realized that the fall equinox was six days away.

Last time, she'd started dreaming about the Riprap man a week before the solstice.

He was coming for her again, either on the night of the equinox, or more likely, the night after.

Why hadn't he come for her friends before now? It was why the other witches didn't want anything to do with her. The few witches who had escaped him before her had been ostracized because the Riprap man had cursed them. The bad luck of the witch who had survived eddied out around her, affecting every other witch they came in contact with.

The dream had let her know that the Riprap man didn't care about her friends, or the rest of her coven.

He was focused on her.

The Riprap man was yet again coming for her soul.

And she didn't have any idea how to escape this time.

CHAPTER 2

Finding a witch in this modern city of Portland has been easier than I'd expected. Of course, they were part of that disgusting suffragist movement. Though I've seen witches with extraordinary power, none of them are the match for any male practitioner. However, the first one was quite clever. Unlike a man, who would be brave enough to seek his fate alone, the damned witch brought her entire coven of sisters. Only now are they realizing what a mistake that was. I haunt the full coven now. Soon enough, they will turn their collective backs on the one who has brought them such bad luck. They may call themselves sisters, but I will break the bonds they've forged together, turn them against one other. Once that is accomplished, the rest will be easy.

Wilson Evermore, Witch Hunter and Chief Magician, 1901

. . .

Tara had managed to get back to sleep after she'd finished her tea, much to her surprise. Though her dreams didn't contain any more hauntings, she still woke up tired.

She wasn't surprised to find a note from Kyle on the kitchen counter, asking what was wrong. He'd woken up while she was having her tea, and so knew that something was up.

What could she tell him, though? *The Riprap man comes for me next Wednesday, on the equinox?* While that might be accurate, it seemed a bit melodramatic. She finally settled on texting him, *Bad dream. Talk more later*.

And she would talk with him. He'd been there to take care of her, watch over her physical body while her soul had battled the Riprap man. She'd never wanted to have to do that again. It had taken her time to recover, as if she'd gone through a long illness. Sometimes she still felt as though her soul was no longer fully attached to her body.

Tara went through her usual morning routine, a slow roll into the morning as she liked to call it. It wasn't that she couldn't wake up first thing. She just preferred to take her time rising out of the unconscious to discover her conscious self.

She made herself a salad for breakfast, clipping basil, marjoram, and sorrel from the long row of pots that Kyle let her keep on his balcony. To that, she added pine nuts, bacon, and a poached egg, breaking the yolk so it warmed up the greens and made the dressing creamy. Only after she finished eating did she make herself tea. That morning, she chose a bright green tea, adding strawberries, ginger, and a touch of cinnamon to liven up her senses, along with a touch of buckwheat honey.

When her tea had finished steeping, Tara went out and sat on the uncomfortable metal chairs that Kyle had out on his balcony. His view showed the courtyard of the condo, a very small green area six stories below, but mostly just the buildings on the other side. She *missed* her river view, even if the river was perilous for her. Water was still her element.

Kyle's place had been wonderful. A great port for her to rest in while she had tried to get her life together.

But it was really past time for her to get moving. Just because that asshole—the Riprap man—was haunting her again didn't mean she couldn't start moving forward.

She realized as she sipped her tea that she'd been in a holding pattern, afraid of exactly what had happened, that the Riprap man would come back to haunt her.

Now that she knew he was there, coming for her again, it was time for her to get on with her life. She wasn't sure why it worked that way, but it appeared to.

How was she going to defeat him? This wasn't like the previous times that he'd taken a witch's soul. Did he still think that he needed to bind her to the Burnside Bridge? The bridge had already been reopened, without a witch's soul. Was this just for revenge? Or was there some other reason he was stalking her again?

Tara had too many questions. She could ask Aaloka, though she wasn't sure she could trust her former teacher's answers. She could also talk with Miss Lucy, who at least wouldn't lie to her.

And who else did she want to recruit for a coven? *Her* coven, though it was still uncomfortable for her to think along those lines.

Richard, though he couldn't stand in any of the circles. Or could he? Would having someone mundane spoil the magic of the circle? Did he have to have power? Was he even interested? Did she want to invite him when there was potential danger?

Kyle, who wouldn't abandon her. Tara had never had such a good friend before. She now had a much better idea of what she wanted in a partner—some of Kyle's better tendencies, as well as some of Richard's.

Ginny—if Tara could find her again.

That left two more for Tara to find. Possibly before the equinox. How did one find disenfranchised witches? Advertise on Meetup? Or should she look at a dating site?

Tara suddenly felt as overwhelmed as when she'd tried looking for work. There were too many options, too many things she didn't know. Too many pieces she had to piece together.

She knew what would settle her the best: a long swim, down at the Y. It was why the river spirit had spared her. He'd grown tired of the Riprap man and wanted someone like her to honor him. She had an affinity for the water, unlike the Riprap man.

How could Tara move forward? How could she beat him? What was she going to do with the rest of her life?

She needed a direction, something more to live for, more than ever.

But what?

TARA MET WITH AALOKA AT THEIR USUAL SPOT, URBAN Tea, northwest of downtown in the neighborhood called *Uptown*, close to the vegan bakery that Aaloka liked to visit. The shop made their own flavored teas, and had one hundred and fifty different varieties. Tara had met Philip, the tea master, and the pair of them had geeked out over ingredients more than once.

That day, Tara had their Hi-Berry tea, a mixture of hibiscus, raspberry, and ginger. She might have added a touch of rose hips, to flatten it out some, but Philip wasn't there for her to make the suggestion to.

The tea shop was crowded for a Friday, students lounging at tables with headphones on and books scattered across their tables, taking up as much space as they could without being rude about it. The inside seating of the shop was always too dim for Tara, and she didn't really know how the students could read in such light. The pre-mixed teas were stacked in rows behind the counter, color-coded to indicate the type of tea.

Next to the teas stood three huge stainless steel containers that held the water the shop needed, each precisely kept at a different temperature, depending on the type of tea. Tara envied the shop's precision. Her electric tea pot had a thermostat in it so she could keep track of temperature; however, it wasn't that accurate.

Quiet indie pop played from the speakers, some band that Tara wouldn't recognize even if she tried. She just wasn't that hip. The smell of cranberry scones filled the space, the special of the day, served warm with clotted cream.

Tara had thought about applying to work at the tea shop, but she knew it would drive her crazy to have to serve someone else's teas. She would have always been wanting to add or subtract ingredients, to serve people the exact perfect tea that they were craving, even if they didn't know it.

In her ideal world, Tara would have enough money to open up her own tea shop. She wouldn't have prepared teas, or there might be a few standards. But for the most part, it would be bespoke tea, each cup hand crafted for that individual's needs.

However, she wasn't sure that would fly, even in hipster Portland.

Tara took her cup outside to sit at one of the sidewalk tables while she waited for Aaloka. A dingy white umbrella held off most of the bright sunlight beating down from the clear blue sky. Young people marched up and down on the sidewalk, coming back from school, heading off to their second or third job.

Damn it. Everyone was working but her. Why hadn't she found something yet?

Aaloka was late, as usual. As she'd once told Tara, she had been born with a loose relationship with time. But at least she wasn't too late this time, merely fifteen minutes. Tara had only just finished her first cup and had started contemplating her second.

"Tara! So good to see you!" Aaloka said as she came rushing forward, taking Tara's hands and squeezing them tightly.

Aaloka always greeted Tara that way. Was she at one point expecting that Tara wouldn't be there?

"Good to see you, too," Tara said.

Though Aaloka was petite, maybe standing only five feet tall, her personality always seemed so huge to Tara. Aaloka wore a beautiful matching lavender skirt and jacket, the color perfectly setting off her dark skin and black hair. While Aaloka had been raised in Sri Lanka, she only tended to wear saris for formal occasions.

Tara sat and waited while Aaloka went to go get her drink, though she returned with one of the scones for them to share.

Tara didn't really eat a lot of grain, which Aaloka knew. However, the other woman never seemed to remember.

"So tell me what has you so gloomy," Aaloka declared after portioning off the scone, handing Tara a tiny piece as requested.

Tara had debated what she would say to her former teacher all afternoon.

The moment was now.

"The Riprap man is back," Tara said.

Aaloka's dark eyes grew huge. "Really?" she asked, sounding breathless.

Tara nodded. "Yes. Seems his new date for taking my soul is the equinox, next week."

"Oh. Oh!" Aaloka said. "I'd thought—hoped—that he would let you be. That he'd let *us* be."

"Has he started bothering the other witches in the coven?" Tara asked. Surely someone would have said something. Or had he just started?

"Sheila claimed that he came to visit her in a dream last night, warning her against helping you," Aaloka admitted. "I…I hadn't believed her."

"What? Why?" Tara asked, confused. Aaloka would never stand up to Sheila, the head of her former coven. Though Aaloka had been angry at Sheila for cheating Tara of her proper place, she hadn't quit the coven. In the end, only Kyle had quit, along with Tara.

"Sheila says a lot of things," Aaloka said quietly. "Things that I know are not true." She shrugged. "I know you're a better person than who she claims you are. It is part of why we meet every week. So that I can see you, see the real you, not the boogieman that Sheila has made you into."

Tara opened her mouth then shut it closed again, her teeth landing together so hard they clicked. What was Sheila saying? And why would Aaloka just listen, and not actually say anything?

"Do I have a target on my back?" Tara asked, not bothering to hide the anger in her voice. "Are the other witches in the coven coming for me? As well as the damned Riprap man?"

"Shh, no, don't be silly," Aaloka said, glancing around.

Tara fumed. "Then what are the other witches going to do? Is Sheila going to suggest that I have an *accident* or something? That whatever bad luck falls my way is well deserved?"

Aaloka kept her lips pressed together tightly for a moment, all the blood leaving the pink flesh, before she finally spoke. "Sheila would never do something as foolish as that. You may not believe me, but I wouldn't allow such a thing. You left the coven, cut your ties. The Riprap man won't cause us harm as a way to pressure you."

"But he will try to hurt those around me," Tara said. "Or at least, that's always been his pattern."

"Since the first witches that he's claimed, yes. He has turned sister against sister," Aaloka admitted.

"When did he take his first witch?" Tara asked.

"We believe 1900 or so," Aaloka said. "It's never been that many witches. Just one here or there."

"Coinciding with the repair or rebuilding of any of the bridges," Tara supplied.

"Yes," Aaloka said. "I've been trying to learn about him, to look at the old texts, so that I could tell you. If he came back."

Tara thought for a moment. What the hell. "I'm forming my own coven," she said. "To fight him."

Aaloka blinked at her. "Really? Do you think that's wise?"

Tara shrugged. "He hasn't come after anyone else I knew. I don't believe he'll come after the others. He's changed. The battle with the river god left him weakened."

"And you promised to honor the river spirit with rose petals on the equinox, right?" Aaloka said.

Tara nodded, surprised that her old teacher had remembered. "That's correct."

"It's a trap," Aaloka announced suddenly.

"What?" Tara asked, confused.

"You can't go anywhere near the water," Aaloka said. "The further away from it, the better."

"You think I should run away? That I could run away this time?" Tara said. That hadn't even occurred to her, quite frankly.

"Yes," Aaloka said. "Run far and fast. It's no longer 1900. You have options, and can get away. He only has power here."

"But will he come after the others if I do leave?" Tara said. She could go and visit her parents back in Wisconsin for a while…

"I don't know," Aaloka said. She reached across the table and squeezed Tara's hand tightly. "I just know that in my heart, I wish you safely gone."

Tara nodded, understanding her former teacher's sentiment.

Even after Aaloka had left, Tara stayed sitting at the table, the afternoon throwing long, dark shadows along the street. People rushed along the sidewalk, scurrying to their homes and safe corners. The air had changed, and now smelled of a coming storm.

Or maybe that was just Tara being haunted again.

Should she go? Would everyone be safer if she did?

And if she did leave, could she ever come back?

TARA HAD A LONG TALK WITH KYLE THAT NIGHT OVER dinner, telling him everything: the dream, her conversation with Aaloka, thinking about a coven as well as considering leaving Portland.

Kyle had changed into his weekend clothes, a black Hawaiian style shirt with bright yellow sunflowers scattered across it, jeans, and bare feet. He wouldn't start wearing long sleeved shirts until it had grown much colder. The air still carried the promise of rain, and the temperature had dropped considerably.

They'd finished eating (leftover meatloaf from Tuesday with a huge salad) and now sat drinking their special brews of tea. Tara had mixed up a large batch of ingredients for Kyle so he could always make his own tea, with licorice, mint, chicory, and roasted dandelion roots—a hearty brew that was a good substitute for coffee in the evenings. She preferred something lighter and sweeter, as well as calming, and so had chamomile, peppermint, wintergreen, cacao nibs, and dried apple bits, with a splash of homemade vanilla.

They sat together on the leather couch, the material warming slowly. They'd lowered the lights in the living room so they could see outside, watch the clouds gathering.

It was cozy, but not. Tara was always careful to keep a formal distance between her and Kyle. He'd never been comfortable with physical touch—he'd been gang raped in his youth and still had both physical and psychological scars.

"I think," Kyle started after sitting in silence for some time, "that leaving doesn't make much sense.

Since the Riprap man probably doesn't want your soul for a bridge, it doesn't matter where you are. He's a supernatural being. He can probably find you wherever you go."

Tara had come to the same conclusion earlier. "I am still going to talk to my mom about them getting me a ticket to go see them," she said. It had become so much more important, suddenly.

"That's a good idea," Kyle said. "Family's important," he added, throwing her a smile.

Tara gave him warm smile in return. She didn't know much about Kyle's parents, except that they lived somewhere on the east coast and didn't necessarily approve of their son's lifestyle. Kyle had talked about the importance of found family more than once.

She felt blessed that he considered her part of it.

"As for creating your own coven, you know I think that's a good idea," he said. "Talk with Ginny tomorrow. And with Richard. Let's see if we can gather together on the night of the equinox."

Tara snorted at him. "No pressure, right?"

Kyle shrugged. "I may, *may*, have another being that I'd like to suggest for a spot. I need to contact them first."

Tara was intrigued by his word choice. *Being*, not *person*.

Though Tara had been taught by her mentors that there were other beings of power, not necessarily human, she'd never been introduced to one. She'd always assumed it was because she wasn't powerful enough to handle such a being if they took a disliking to her.

Still, Tara knew better than to question Kyle. He wouldn't say anything until he was damned good and ready.

"I'm having dinner with Richard tomorrow night," Tara said eventually. Hopefully he wouldn't be too freaked out by her and her magic that he'd stop wanting to be her friend.

"He'll be fine," Kyle said, reading her worry.

"I hope so," Tara said. What would she do if she lost yet another friend? She still felt as though she'd lost too much already.

"Come," Kyle said, standing up. He actually held out a hand for her to take.

Tara did so, distrusting what her friend was up to.

"Let's do some magic," he said with a sly grin after he squeezed her hand and released it.

"Okay," Tara said slowly, though her heart leaped. Magic! She'd been practicing, but as Kyle had said to her earlier, she was a witch who preferred working with a coven, not being on her own.

Kyle led the way out to the balcony, stacking the chairs up and shoving the table to one side so they had more room.

"Won't the neighbors see us?" Tara asked, confused. She'd kept her practice indoors, though she preferred being outside.

In response, Kyle went inside, rooted around in one of the living room cupboards, then came out again, bearing three sachets that he carefully placed on the balcony railing. "For protection," he said, "distraction, and invisibility."

The small bags looked nothing like Tara's usual sachets. Instead of being made out of plain cotton, these were crafted out of black leather, blue silk, and a green-and-gold brocade. Each one was the size of a small dinner plate, though bulky, as if stuffed with herbs and other ingredients. She could smell the magic they contained, a dark sweet note that touched the roof of her mouth.

"Cool," Tara said, making a mental note to ask Kyle about the exact ingredients he'd used. Then she paused, thought for a moment. "Why didn't you tell me about these sooner?"

Kyle shrugged sheepishly. "I figured you could make your own. I know, I know, you don't think you're capable. But you're a lot stronger than you realize."

"I'm still only a witch of the first circle, of thought," Tara reminded him.

"And that's something we're going to have to fix," he said. "You and I both know that you're worthy of the second circle."

"But we don't have a meditation circle," Tara said, confused. Both Miss Lucy's coven as well as Sheila's coven had meditation circles that an initiate had to travel through in order to move within, tests to pass to go from one circle to the next.

"There are other ways to advance," Kyle said. "Do you trust me?"

Tara stood up straighter. "I do," she said. "With my life, my soul, and all my magic."

The smile that Kyle gave her brightened up the dark porch. "Then let's begin."

~

KYLE LED THE STARTING PRAYERS, AS THIS WAS HIS place and his circle. Tara listened more closely than she usually did, knowing that someday, possibly sooner rather than later, she was going to be the one leading the circle.

They stood in the center of the darkened balcony, protected from curious or spying eyes by Kyle's magic and his sachets. They both stood barefoot: Even though they stood on concrete rather than dirt, Kyle insisted that they needed to feel the earth with their bare skin. Their hands were linked, but with only a single finger, as Kyle still didn't like being touched more than necessary.

"We thank the goddess Brigid, defender of the earth, for allowing us this space and time on Her plane," Kyle intoned.

Gone was the goofy guy who'd teased her about purposefully cutting up too many vegetables for dinner so that he'd be forced to eat the extras. The person who stood in front of her was a powerful orator with a presence that easily filled the small balcony. He would have made an impressive lawyer, appealing to the jury on behalf of his client.

Maybe that was part of why he worked behind the scenes—so that he wouldn't have to give persuasive arguments for clients he didn't believe in.

Even his bright Hawaiian shirt looked more formal, the yellow flowers like globes of armor across his chest.

Kyle continued. "We ask the god Samil, warrior for the people, to watch over us in the rightness of our deeds. May the old mother moon send her light and knowledge, for Hayvu and Eural to carry their justice to us on their winds. Finally, may Areebin, the protector of souls, guide us fairly to the summer lands, but only in the fairness of time."

Then Kyle started one of the older hymns that Tara had learned, about the fullness of time and the turning of the seasons. It was appropriate for the time of year, when summer still hadn't given up, though fall was bearing down on them hard.

Tara was pleased with how nicely her alto voice went with Kyle's lighter baritone. She'd expected him to be a bass, but was surprised to find that his voice, while mid-tone, was rich.

When they'd finished, Tara looked expectantly at Kyle, unsure what he had in mind.

From one of the back pockets of his jeans, Kyle fished out a tiny glass bottle. It was maybe two inches long, with an elaborate silver filigreed stopper that was almost as big as the bottle. Kyle bent over and placed it on the floor between them.

Even from where she was standing, Tara felt the power of the small bottle. It wasn't any bigger than her palm, but it bristled with energy. She nearly jumped when a single light blinked off and on, inside it, as though it had captured a tiny firefly.

More lights joined the first, yellowish and each as small as a pea. They seemed agitated.

"Where did you get this?" Tara asked, impressed. "And how did you hide it?"

Kyle grinned at her. "That cupboard is protected," he said simply. "You've never even been curious about what it contained."

Tara nodded, her eyes wide. "That's true. You enspelled it? Wow."

Kyle shrugged. "Mainly just made it a sacred space for my belongings. It kind of protects itself."

"I don't understand," Tara said. It was awfully difficult to permanently enchant anything. The spells had to be renewed often. Even if the item was handcrafted with magic, it still wouldn't "hold" the power channeled into it.

"Sacred spaces can be despoiled," Kyle said seriously. "But it takes effort. First you have to gain access. A space that's been dedicated to a specific person or group can gain an awareness, and provide some level of protection for itself."

"Okay," Tara said. She'd never even heard of such a thing. Though now that she thought about it, she had always wondered about the backyard that contained the meditation maze that the witches walked when moving from one circle to the next. The space had always felt isolated, cut off from the rest of the city. Maybe that was its way of protecting itself.

She looked back down at the glass bottle that still sparked between them. "What are we supposed to do with that?" she asked.

"That's a captured wind," Kyle said with a grin. "Oh, don't worry. It's tiny. But for your test to see if you can pass within, to the circle of air, let's see if you can tame this wind."

Tara gasped. "But how can you…how did you…what?"

"You're not the only one with powers," Kyle told her sternly. "And I've been preparing for this, for when you were ready to start fully practicing again."

Tara shivered. Kyle was right. Part of why she hadn't been moving forward was because her magic still felt raw, as if all the skin had been scraped off. She'd needed time to heal before she could start practicing again.

"Are you sure I'm ready?" Tara had to ask. Because she wasn't.

Kyle shrugged. "If you are ready, this will be a breeze, no pun intended. If you aren't ready, we can wait and try again in a few weeks."

Tara nodded. She understood why he was doing this. It would give her a great deal of confidence if she could do this. And it wouldn't completely break her if she couldn't.

"All right," Tara said after taking a few deep breaths. She readied her prayers and focused her powers, calling on the winds to protect her, as well as reaching deep inside herself for her own fire. "Let's do this."

"Blessed be," Kyle said, the words ringing out as if they formed a circle of protection around her.

"Blessed be," Tara acknowledged. She put the heels

of her hands together, the fingers outstretched, as if she was an anime character, ready to catch a fireball.

Kyle crouched down and put one hand on the bottle, one hand on the stopper. Then he looked back up at her.

When Tara nodded, he slowly pulled the stopper up.

With a loud *pop*, the stopper came loose.

And the winds poured out.

Tara tensed as the winds flowed up, past her, seeking a way off the closed balcony. But Kyle had enfolded the space, so nothing could escape. She jerked her hands back when stinging lightning tickled her palms. Anger rose, as did the familiar exhaustion.

She wasn't ready for this. She would never be ready for this. Hadn't she already failed before? Must she fail so publicly again?

With an abrupt shake of her head, Tara pushed the negative thoughts away. Where had that come from? It had *not* been her fault that she'd failed the first circle walk.

Winds brushed the back of her neck, stirring her short ponytail. Tara forced her shoulders down as she followed the circling winds. They pushed, cackling, to the far corner, then back again, like a puppy racing to all the interesting parts of a room, then coming back to share *everything*.

They weren't trying to escape, weren't desperate or angry. Not like she'd expected them to be.

In fact, if Tara was any judge, she'd say that the winds wanted to *play*.

Tara paused. When was the last time she'd played?

With a jerk of her hand, Tara freed her hair from its

usual ponytail. The winds picked up the strands immediately, tugging on them. She rolled her head, then stretched her arms out. Winds raced across her chest, to her fingers and back, again, like a puppy nosing her skin, learning all her different smells.

When Tara brought her arms down slowly, she brought the winds with her, until she was holding a ball of joyous frolicking energy, like a wiggling dog that was trying to lick her face while getting all its skin scratched at the same time.

The winds raced around and around the balcony when she let them go. Tara laughed at Kyle's grin.

So how to tame them?

Tara blew out a breath, then she blew again, aiming upward.

The wind rushed forward, trying to tangle with Tara's breath.

Tara sucked in abruptly as the wind brushed against her face in its haste, taking deep inside of her a bit of the wind. It tasted cold, like April rains, with a hint of lavender thrown in. Or maybe that was purple heather.

Tara raised up her arms and started circling her hands in front of her, like she was spinning two large disks. The winds drew closer again, following her movements, twirling themselves around and around, like two mini cyclones.

After a few more moments of dancing with the winds, Tara spread her hands up and down, scooping up the bottom of the wind and pushing it together, compressing it like a spongy ball. It was the first time she'd felt some resistance—the wind didn't want to be tamed. But it settled down after a few moments, compressing down into a cackling sphere, about the size of a basketball, in between her hands.

Tara caressed the ball, calming it, before she looked up at Kyle. "Now what?" she asked.

Kyle snorted at her. "I have no idea. I've never seen someone work with the wind like that before. Certainly not someone who is merely first level. Winds aren't that friendly with me. Maybe you should tell me what's next."

Tara blinked at him. What was he talking about? Surely everyone managed balls of wind like this.

"Uhm," Tara said, glancing down at the ball she still held. The wind didn't like being compressed like this for long. She'd have to direct it or release it, soon.

"Let it hunt," Tara said after a moment. "I need to find Ginny, right? So why not see if the wind will hunt for me."

"Okay," Kyle said slowly, as if he'd never heard of such a thing. He picked up the middle charm from the balcony.

Tara could tell where the hole had opened, like an iris of gray across a darker black shade. She held the image of Ginny as firmly as she could in her head before she tossed the ball of wind through the hole. "Go find her," she commanded.

It leaped out of her hands, elongating into a sleek black greyhound as it flowed away, out into the night.

Tara glanced at Kyle, curious if he'd just seen the wind change into a dog or not. From the way his eyebrows rested at the top of his forehead, she figured he had.

"Will it find Ginny?" Kyle asked.

Tara shrugged. "It will try. I think."

Kyle shook his head, then held out his hands.

Curious, Tara took them, holding on with just pinkies, as usual.

"I hereby acknowledge that you have passed within, and proclaim you a full witch of the second circle, the circle of air," Kyle announced.

A shiver of magic passed between them, electricity tickling Tara's palms again. She gasped, unsure of what spell Kyle had just done.

But she felt it. Felt the difference. Something inside of her was now *free* to work with the wind and the air, as if she'd been blocked before and had never realized it, like looking through a dirty window that was suddenly clean.

"Wow," Tara said.

Kyle nodded. "I wasn't sure it would work," he admitted. "But I thought it was worth trying. You *should* have been allowed to pass the first time. You were more than ready."

"Can you teach me that?" Tara said, "How to acknowledge a new witch?"

"I can," Kyle said solemnly. "Realize, though, that you can only pass someone within who is at a lower level than yourself. Plus, normally, I'd warn you that not all witches have the ability. They need to supplement with potions and such. But I think you won't have a problem."

Tara shrugged, uncomfortable with the praise. "I might," she said.

Kyle snorted at her. "And now, I think it's time for a good bottle of wine and some bad 1970s sitcoms. You game?"

"Absolutely!" Tara said, happy to put aside the magic for a while, to recover in the snark and goofiness of a good friend.

And Kyle never said anything, even though Tara found her attention drawn again and again to the windows filled with night and the occasional breeze.

CHAPTER 3

I may have miscalculated. There appear to be two classes of witches: those who are called 'schooled witches' who travel within, going from one circle of power to the next, and the 'hedgewitches' who have natural magic. The latter are generally not associated with a coven, but work on their own. While frequently an entire coven will attempt to fight me, they learn quickly to turn against the one I've chosen rather than battle the misfortune I bring to them. I had considered that it might be easier to go after one of the singular witches instead. However, their magic is too dissimilar to mine. We appear to be at a standstill. And the deadline for completion of the next bridge is approaching. I need to either finish her off, or choose another. And quickly.

Wilson Evermore, Chief Magician and Protector of Portland, 1905

CLOUDS and gray skies greeted Tara the next morning. She woke restless, needing to move from sleep to waking faster than usual, and finished with her morning tea just as Kyle came back from his run instead of just starting breakfast.

Tara nodded over her shoulder at him but didn't try to say anything. It was one of the reasons why she needed to find someplace else to live. While Kyle was lovely, and certainly supportive of her, there was a reason why he lived alone, and she always had flatmates, people she could talk with whenever they came into the room.

Tara made a second cup of tea—this time no caffeine, just rooibos, spearmint, lavender and lemon verbena, a bright, sweet mix—and was quietly sipping it when Kyle came out to join her. She had on jeans, thick socks, a plain red T-shirt, with an oversized soft, gray wool shirt over it. She'd stolen the baggy shirt from her dad. It felt good to dig into her suitcases and pull out a few of her warmer pieces. The summer had been weird, long, and hot.

Over his jeans, Kyle wore a University of Washington gray sweatshirt, something he'd picked up when he'd gone to law school there. He'd mentioned once that while he had the grades to go to one of the more prestigious law schools on the east coast, he didn't want to be that close to his family. He carried his own coffee mug.

Tara wished yet again that coffee tasted as good as it smelled, but it never did.

"You're up early," Kyle commented after he'd sat

down and they'd enjoyed a moment of quiet between them.

"Restless," Tara admitted.

"Bad dreams?" Kyle asked. He didn't look over at her, but kept his gaze out on the horizon, as if he could see beyond the ugly block of condos directly across the courtyard from them.

"No," Tara said. "Just woke up and needed to move. Considered going on your run with you."

That got Tara a look. "Really?"

She grinned at him. "Just a brief moment of insanity," she assured him.

Tara didn't like to run. She much preferred to swim and do yoga. Though she had considered doing more physical activities, as she was getting older and it seemed it took more to keep herself in good shape.

"Good," Kyle said. "Or else I would have wondered if the Riprap man had already taken your soul and replaced it with someone else's."

"Yeah," Tara acknowledged. She still didn't have any idea how she was going to fight the Riprap man. At least last time she'd been working toward the next level of witchcraft, and so had a plan. Even if it had backfired.

This time, she really didn't have a clue, beyond trying to form her own coven.

"Feel different this morning?" Kyle asked after a few more moments of comfortable silence.

Tara paused, probing. "I don't feel stronger," she said. "My power didn't grow with the ceremony last night. I still feel clearer, though. As if all the cobwebs have been brushed away."

Kyle nodded. He appeared to be choosing his words carefully. "I wasn't sure what you'd feel, which is why I didn't warn you about anything. I can only tell you what I was told, and how I felt."

Tara smiled at him, encouraging him to speak. It was a different form of intimacy, to share this sort of knowledge, and Kyle still had difficulty with that.

"For me, I felt as though the line of power coming from my core had suddenly doubled, going from being a single wire to being two. I did feel much stronger, as do most. My guess is that you already had the power, you should have been passed within at the original ceremony. All I did was clear the path for you."

He paused, taking a sip of his coffee, before he continued. "My other assumption is that you're probably already capable of passing further inward. That you don't need to do a lot of work before you pass into the circle of fire."

"Really?" Tara asked, surprised. "But I don't know all the lore for that level yet!"

Kyle snorted. "Not sure you need it," he said. "I still think you're a hedgewitch, one who works with elements directly instead of herbs and knowledge. Just your power should be enough."

"I'll think about it," Tara said. It would give her a focus, to start studying again. "After the equinox," she added. She didn't want to have to split her attention again, like she had the last time, working so hard to pass a test that was snatched out from under her at the last moment.

"All right," Kyle said slowly. He paused again before he asked, "So what is the plan today?"

"I'm going to the Saturday market, to see if I can find Ginny," Tara said.

"Want some company?" Kyle said.

"That would be awesome," Tara said. She never assumed that he would want to go anywhere with her; he still had his own life and friends, apart from her.

"Then let's go," Kyle said.

Before Tara could spring up from her seat, he added, "After I finish my coffee."

With an exaggerated sigh, Tara sat back in her chair, pouting. She really did feel antsy, wanting to go.

"Have you heard from that tamed wind of yours?" Kyle asked after a moment.

"No," Tara said. "Honestly, it's felt as if the wind almost returned a few times. But then it would go chasing off after a new scent again. It's still a puppy, and not trained."

"I see," Kyle said. He looked at her and shrugged. "I have no experience with this whatsoever. You're kind of on your own when it comes to having a tame wind who's kind of like a dog."

"I don't know either," Tara said. She'd planned on asking Richard later that evening, when she went out to dinner with him. He'd respected her request to meet him alone, as Tara hadn't wanted to have to try to explain all the witchcraft to yet another outsider. At least, not yet.

Finally, Kyle finished his coffee. Tara felt like a

puppy herself who'd been promised a walk when he announced that he was ready.

Was this going to be her natural state from now on? Gods, she hoped not.

❀

THE SMELL OF MINI-DONUTS DREW TARA AND KYLE forward. Tara tried not to eat that much grain or junk food; however, the scent of fried dough and cinnamon sugar was still mouthwatering.

Though the Saturday market had only just opened, people were already in line at the front booths. Late tourists? Or locals already shopping for both Halloween as well as Christmas?

Then Tara realized both booths sold coffee. Of course, there were lines.

Could she open up a tea shop here? What would be involved with that? What sort of permits would she have to get? Could she survive just being open on the weekends? And would a town like Portland support another tea shop?

All questions for tomorrow.

If that silly wind of hers had returned by now, she might have asked it to go searching for Ginny. Instead, Tara and Kyle walked down the brick street, peering at the booths first on one side, then the other. What sort of booth would Ginny be at? Tara assumed it would be smaller, not the shop with hundreds of angel candle holders, or the one with row after row of necklaces and trinkets. But more like the shop with all the paintings done by a single artist, or even the shop that sold hand-blown glass ornaments and offered free lessons.

What sort of glass could Tara make, if she managed to pass within to the circle of fire? Was that even possible? She'd have to remember to ask Kyle later.

After wandering up and down the aisles both on the outdoor part of the market (with separate booths) and the indoor part (covered and too crowded for both of them) Tara felt something tugging on her attention.

She stopped and turned.

Out of the corner of her eye, Tara saw a black shape —no, a black greyhound, long and thin—glancing over his shoulder at her, then racing away, toward the outside booths.

"This way," Tara said, walking quickly in that direction.

Kyle followed without a word.

Tara wove herself through the crowds, which now all seemed to be coming from the direction she wanted to go in, like a salmon swimming upstream. It was odd. As soon as she saw a clear path, more people would block her way.

Frustrated after only taking a few steps, only to be forced to turn to the side again, Tara called up a spark of fire. It wasn't enough to set her skin glowing. People weren't suddenly going to brush against her and catch on fire, or even feel the heat.

The crowds now parted for her. The area was still overly full (and where had all those people come from?). However, Tara made forward progress.

Out in the open, past the covered area, Tara saw the dog again. He appeared to be looking for her.

There was no question that it was the same dog from last night, her personal wind, taken animal shape.

However, she would also swear that he'd doubled in size since the previous night. While he was still a puppy and had a young face, his body had grown considerably, and he now came up to her knee. Black fur had grown richer, making him seem more like a shadow. His dark eyes gazed at her with considerable intelligence. His ears were flopped down, but rose up to fine points when he saw her again. He gave her a nod, then turned and raced away again.

"Did you see that?" Tara asked Kyle as he came up behind her.

"See what?" Kyle said. "See that dog? That tamed wind of yours? Yeah, I saw him."

He didn't sound pleased. Tara wasn't sure why. "I bet he's found Ginny," Tara said defensively.

"I'm sure of it." Kyle pressed his lips together as if to prevent himself from saying more.

Why was the dog making Kyle nervous? Tara was going to have to ask about that later. "Come on," she said, walking forward.

Kyle stayed a few feet back, behind Tara, and to her right. Why wasn't he walking beside her?

It took Tara a few steps to realize that Kyle was in a defensive position. If they were facing a strong witch, he wouldn't be blasted first thing. No, just Tara would. While anyone trying to sneak up on her would be facing him.

Tara squared her shoulders and reached for the sachet in her pocket. She focused on herbs to help her see clearly, such as red raspberry, fennel, and ginko, as well as cloves and nettle for protection. She squeezed the sachet, willing the power of the herbs to aid her.

There. The crowds in front of her finally parted. Sitting at a small table, not even a proper booth, Tara caught a glimpse of bright red hair. Beside her sat another woman with dark brown hair.

This time, Tara would not be deterred. She called up more of her fire, making herself a force that people unconsciously turned away from, before she marched forward.

The table was small, barely big enough for the two chairs behind it. On the right side stood rows of homemade soaps, with beautiful swirling colors through the bars, each wrapped in a hand-labeled tag. The other side of the table had half a dozen mason jars filled with various dried herbs, like spearmint, oregano, sage, thyme, lemon balm, and rose hips.

Ginny looked up as if she faced her doom. The other girl leaned back, making it clear that this wasn't her fight.

"Look, I ain't bothering ye," Ginny said, exasperated. "Why can't you jist leave us alone?"

Tara stopped, bewildered. "I'm sorry?" she said. "I don't understand. I was looking for you so we could talk."

"Oh," Ginny said. "Ye aren't trying to order me out of yer territory?"

"What?" Tara said, shocked. "Territory? What are you talking about?"

"Some *people* who are 'schooled' don't like us who are home taught," Ginny said, sticking her chin up defiantly.

It took Tara a moment to translate what Ginny had said. Evidently some "schooled" witches didn't like hedgewitches.

She was going to have to ask Aaloka about that, as Kyle had never mentioned anything about some sort of feud between the various schools of witchcraft. Or possibly Miss Lucy, as her former mentor wouldn't lie to her, not ever.

"Though I'm 'schooled,' as it were, I've been told that I'm more like you," Tara said quietly.

Ginny nodded. "So that was your wee beastie following me this morning?"

Something cold suddenly struck Tara's left hand, as if a small fan had just turned on, then shut itself off again.

When Tara looked down, she saw the dog more clearly. It was as if he'd just stuck his nose into her palm, cold but not wet.

He looked up at her expectantly, as if waiting for a treat.

What sort of dog treats would a tamed wind find acceptable? Tara was going to have to figure that out. In the meanwhile, she met his eyes and smiled at him. "Good boy!" she said earnestly. "You did a really good job. Good boy."

Cautiously, Tara reached out to pet the dog. As her

palm followed the contours of his head, the body solidified. She stroked the sleek, cool fur a few more times before turning back to Ginny.

"He's your first wind," Ginny said knowledgably. "Whatcha gonna name him?"

"Soot," Tara said immediately. She knew it wasn't the most imaginative name—that wasn't her forte. At least it was better than just calling him "dog," or "wind dog," which had been her first inclination.

"How did you know he was a wind? Or my first?" Tara asked.

"Ye schooled witches sure don't know a lot," Ginny said. She glanced at her silent companion, who shrugged. "I'm gonna take a break, and come back with more coffee," she announced.

That made her friend smile and nod.

"Come on," Ginny said, coming out from behind the table.

"Uhmmm," Tara said, turning toward Kyle.

He made a shooing motion with his hand. "You two talk. There will be time for introductions later."

"Thanks," Tara said.

Ginny looked between the pair of them before she turned and walked away. Tara quickly joined her. Soot followed her for a few steps, then melted into the crowd, following some scent or another.

"That your boyfriend?" Ginny asked.

"Who, Kyle? No," Tara said firmly. "He's my best friend. And also a schooled witch."

"Haven't seen a lot of guys in the circles," Ginny said.

"Only about a third in any coven are men," Tara said. "They aren't drawn to the craft like women are." She wasn't about to get into the long, involved arguments that she'd had with Kyle about the socialization of boys and why community building and working together with others had never appealed to men.

"Let me tell you a bit about myself," Tara said as they passed into the more formal areas of the market. "I quit my coven earlier this year because the leader cheated on one of my tests, so I couldn't pass. I had a supernatural creature hunting me, who's now come back. Kyle, my friend back there, thinks I'm a hedgewitch and that I need to form my own coven to fight the creature. With different witches in it, not just the schooled variety." Tara took a deep breath then blew it all out again. "I think that covers me. In a nutshell. How about you?"

Ginny snorted at her. "Quite a bit to just drop on someone, don't you think?" Then she held up her hand before Tara could apologize. "Sounds as though yer looking for help. And for members to join yer coven. Eh?"

"Yes. Exactly," Tara said. It wasn't the sort of conversation that she'd imagined having while walking through the crowds at the Saturday market.

Then again, no one appeared to be paying any attention to them. In fact, people kept turning away from the pair of them. It was as if Tara and Ginny walked together in their own separate bubble, apart.

Was she doing that? Or was Ginny?

"Tell me more about this supernatural critter of yers," Ginny said.

Tara told Ginny what she knew of the Riprap man, as well as the final battle, how he'd had to fight the river spirit and how it had changed him. "I don't know why he's coming after me now," Tara said. "Does he want to sacrifice me to a bridge? Is it revenge? Or is this part of a new deal with the river spirit?"

Ginny leaned over and sniffed Tara, then paused for a moment. "Yer a water creature, right?" Ginny said as she started walking forward again.

"I am," Tara said. "Can you smell the water?"

"The chlorine," Ginny admitted. "Ye go to the pool instead of to the beach."

"Ah," Tara said. "And you?" she asked, wondering if that was appropriate or not.

But Ginny didn't bristle at her. "Mostly winds and air," she said as she led them to the back of a long line of customers waiting for their caffeine fix. "Had to let the lot of 'em go when I came across the pond. They wouldn't aben happy 'ere."

"I see," Tara said, though she didn't. Evidently, Soot was a local wind. Good to know.

Would Tara be able to "tame" a water…source? A spring? A river? Or just an element? Like maybe a glass of water? Or a full water bottle? She had no idea.

"I was surprised to see yer wind come sniffing around this morning," Ginny told her confidently. "The schooled witches have lost all the old spells. Oh, it ain't that they're weak. Just got different strengths."

"Can you teach me?" Tara asked. They stepped

forward. The line was moving much more swiftly than Tara had expected. Then she studied the people in line in front of them. Not all of them, but a few appeared to be suddenly called away, either by friends, or as if they'd just decided not to get coffee but maybe a donut instead, the winds carrying the sweet scent to them.

It took Tara a moment to realize this was Ginny's doing. Her winds were culling the people in line.

Clever. Tara was going to have to learn how to do that. Or would she be able to, given that her element was actually water and not air?

"Don't know what I could teach ye," Ginny said. "There's not a lot of formal teaching, ye know. Spells I do, you can't repeat. Different powers. Different people. It's why the schooled witches think they're so much better. Superior, like."

Tara could see that. It was the spirit of the modern age, to be able to repeat something reliably. To make it science, and not, well, witchcraft.

They got to the head of the line. Ginny ordered two large mochas with extra whipped cream, then looked expectantly at Tara.

Tara tried not to appear grudgingly as she pulled out her bank card. But she supposed it was fair, as she was trying to recruit the other woman.

"Don't you want any?" Ginny asked as they went to join the line for picking up their orders.

Tara couldn't help but shudder. "I've tried. But it never tastes as good as it smells, you know? I'd end up adding chocolate and sugar and everything else to it, just to cover the taste." She shrugged. "Would rather drink something that I actually liked. Like tea."

"Make your own?" Ginny said. At Tara's nod, Ginny added, "Whatcha have this morning?"

Tara recognized it as a sort of test. She detailed out the various ingredients of her first cup, starting with an Assam black tea base, then adding dried apple bits, dried ginger, and a few cocoa nibs to smooth it out.

"Huh," Ginny said as they started their walk back, cups in hand. "What about adding some marigold petals?"

Tara shook her head. "That would make it too bright," she said. "I like a darker tea for my first cup."

They discussed various teas and components all the way back to the booth. Tara recognized that they both were hungry to talk herbs with someone else who had the same level of knowledge, someone who they could each bounce ideas off of.

When they were in sight of the booth, Ginny stopped and looked over at Tara. "Now, I'd be daft to join ye and your coven. Ye know that, right? Ye got this creature after ye. The schooled witches don't care much for ye, and may be coming after ye at some point."

"I know," Tara said, swallowing down her disappointment. "But I didn't want to lie to you. Anyone who comes in has to understand the risk. Thank you for talking with me, anyway. And maybe we can go out for tea sometimes, and talk more about herbs and teas later?"

"Jist hold on," Ginny said. "I ain't done. What I was about to say was that me gran always told me to listen to me heart first. So I'll be joining ye and your fancy crew."

"Really?" Tara said, surprised. "Why? It is rather daft, you know."

Ginny grinned at her. "That's what me Gran would have said too. But ye don't leave people in need. Not the ones you connected to." She paused, then continued. "Ye see how all the crowd ignores us?"

Tara nodded. "I figured that was something you were doing."

"Nope," Ginny said. "Tweren't me. Tweren't you, either. It's us."

"But how?" Tara asked, confused. Why didn't this sort of thing happen whenever she was talking with any other witch, like with Kyle?

"Don't know," Ginny said. "Just happens that way." She paused, then added, "Something that drives the schooled witches mad. Magic that just happens. No spell or fancy potion."

"I see," Tara said, nodding. Yes, that would make most of the witches she knew rather crazy.

No wonder the "schooled" witches didn't like the hedgewitches, if magic just happened that way. Or didn't, as it was uncontrollable.

They made plans to meet up again Monday evening, for Ginny to meet Kyle and maybe the other people that Tara had managed to recruit by that point.

"Thank you," Tara said just before she left. Kyle had texted her that he'd already walked back to the apartment.

Ginny gave her a sly grin. "Ye gave me a cause.

Gran always said I needed one, or I'd just drift with me winds."

"You're welcome, then," Tara said.

Ginny nodded, then abruptly gave a sharp whistle.

About twenty feet away, a dark head popped out from between the crowds. Soot, looking at her expectantly.

"Ye'll have to learn how to do that yerself," Ginny said. "Git him to heel."

"I will," Tara said. "Thank you, again."

"Eh, off with ye. I got me work to do," Ginny said. With a final nod of her head, Ginny went back to the booth.

As Tara watched, more people were now blowing their way, Ginny attracting them.

Tara gave a sharp whistle and was pleased to see Soot walking directly toward her.

Good. Maybe training a wind wouldn't be that hard.

TARA'S CHEEKS HURT FROM ALL THE TIMES SHE'D whistled for Soot. He only appeared to hear her and come about half the time. She stood out on Kyle's balcony, sending Soot to fetch things, like a stone she'd tossed from the balcony out into the courtyard below. She had the impression that he could fetch other things as well, but he hadn't managed to bring back the rose she'd asked for. She was more successful when she merely asked for leaves or petals. Still, he ignored her as often as he would come to her.

Was that how accurate a hedgewitch's magic was going to be? That anything she tried would only work about half of the time?

No wonder the schooled witches were so strict in their teachings. While it felt to Tara that their magic wasn't as powerful, it was at least reliable, if you used the right ingredients with the right spell.

Tara walked back into the condo, needing to get ready to go out to dinner with Richard that night. They were going to a hipster hamburger bar that she liked, a place with quiet corners where they could have a chat.

Kyle looked up from the book he was reading. He was sprawled out on the couch, comfortable, with bare feet, jeans, and just a T-shirt. He kept the temperature of the condo warmer than Tara liked, claiming that it was cold enough outside, he didn't need to wear sweaters inside as well.

"Getting ready for your meeting?" Kyle asked.

Tara nodded. "I was lucky with Ginny this morning," she said. "I just hope my luck continues."

"It will," Kyle said firmly. "It's the power of synchronicity. You have a need. The gods and goddesses will provide the people."

Tara smiled at that. Kyle didn't believe in the god he'd been raised with—particularly since that god wouldn't necessarily approve of him or his lifestyle. He did, however, have a small altar to the gods—Samil and Areebin, both protectors—in the corner that he sat in front of and meditated often.

Tara had always kept a very small altar in her bedroom, never out in the living room, as she'd always had roommates who weren't witches. She also didn't worship at her alter. Not exactly.

Unlike her former teacher Aaloka, Tara didn't have as strong a belief in the spirits that moved around them. Tara knew those spirits existed, felt as though she'd actually met wind and water spirits, as well as fire and earth.

Yet, it had never struck her as appropriate to worship them, but rather to honor the spirits. Most of the witches she knew only prayed to the spirits when in a circle.

Tara wasn't sure where she stood with all that. It was yet one more thing she needed to determine if she was going to choose her own path between the schooled witches and being a hedgewitch. Could she carve out a third road?

Tara changed into a clean green blouse and brushed her hair, pulling it back into her usual ponytail. Soot and the winds preferred it when her hair was loose so they could play with it, tug on it and tease her with it. But she wasn't going to need her winds tonight. She didn't bother with makeup, either. First off, it wasn't that sort of date. Second off, she rarely wore makeup anyway. She considered herself pretty enough with wide-spaced blue eyes and clear white skin that had a sprinkling of freckles from the summer sun

No, tonight was a perfectly mundane meeting with a perfectly mundane friend, just meeting for dinner.

A mundane who she was going to ask to join her coven.

Tara realized that she'd hide in her room for the rest of the night if she could rather than go and talk with

Richard. She really didn't want to screw up his friendship. Like Kyle's friendship, it meant a lot to her.

The Riprap man was still hunting her, though. She knew that, even though he hadn't shown up again.

What did he want? How could she defeat him? And would asking Richard to be in her coven actually bring danger to him?

She still had too many questions. And only the faintest of ideas about where her path led.

Tara dug into her "wedgie" burger. The patty was part lamb, part beef, and all delicious, wrapped in a wedge of lettuce with bacon, guacamole, and a sharp cheddar cheese.

Heaven.

Richard was making good progress on his burger as well. He'd gotten a buffalo patty with an egg on it. They shared a basket of garlic-rosemary fries between them.

They'd arrived at the restaurant at the end of the dinner rush, so the tables around them were emptying out as they ate their dinner, the noise level decreasing to more comfortable levels. All the tables were orange plastic, with red plastic seats, but done in fall colors as opposed to bright and obnoxious. The music in the background was some sort of indie pop, a guy singing with a single guitar, so it was easy to ignore.

One of the nice things about the restaurant was that in addition to great burgers and fries, it also served beer, cider, and wine. Tara had a glass of the cucumber hibiscus cider that was as refreshing as tea but with a sweet kick to it, while Richard had a far too bitter triple-hopped beer.

After they'd finished devouring their burgers, they pushed their plates back simultaneously and leaned back.

"Oooof," Richard said as he reached for one of the last remaining fries. "That was good."

"It was," Tara said, nodding. She reached for her drink, trying to pick her words carefully. She had to admit that she just didn't want to say anything. More than a decade of silence was hard to overcome.

"So you said you wanted to see me about something important," Richard said gently, as if trying to break the ice.

Tara threw him a grateful smile. He really was a good guy. Goofy, with black hair that had a few more silver threads running through it than it used to, old-fashioned aviator thick-rimmed glasses hiding pretty hazel eyes, a broad forehead that sloped down to a pointed chin. He looked like the academic that he was, with a red-and-black checkered plaid flannel over the T-shirt that said, "Heisenberg may have slept here."

"I did want to talk with you," Tara said. She took a deep breath. "Look, there isn't any way to say this without just coming out and saying it." She paused again.

"You're pregnant?" Richard guessed. "And Kyle's the father?"

"No!" Tara said, glaring at him.

He grinned impishly.

"No and no," Tara said. She rolled her eyes at him. Richard knew that Kyle was gay, but he still teased her about living with another man. "Look. I'm just going to come out and say this." She sat up straighter, then turned in her seat to face him.

"I'm a witch," she announced.

Richard blinked. "Yeah, I know."

CHAPTER 4

Myths about witches frequently mention cats, especially black cats, as familiars. Yet the schooled witches never keep any animal companions. It turns out that the animal familiars appear to only be associated with the hedgewitches, and carry special powers, such as fire or wind. So while a hedgewitch may be alone, without a coven, she still has gathered her familiars to her, to protect and defend her. What she doesn't realize is that those beasts will be her downfall. I can draw those unnatural creatures to me, more easily than the witch can. She will not see the trap laid before her in her efforts to save her pets.

Wilson Evermore, Witch Hunter and Bridge Protector, 1904

"WHAT DO YOU MEAN, YOU KNOW?" Tara asked, surprised. She'd never told Richard. How had he guessed?

He looked at her, puzzled. "It was kind of obvious," he said. "You celebrate the seasons. You hang out with a group of other people late at night for no apparent reason other than to dance in the moonlight. You know more about herbs and plants than anyone I've ever met, including several Ph.D. level botanists."

"Oh," Tara said slowly. "I guess that makes sense. But…I'm really a witch. I can do magic."

"Duh," Richard said, rolling his eyes at her.

"What?" Tara said, still shocked. "How did you…I don't get it."

With a grin, Richard said, "First off, Miss Lucy was your teacher at the time. If there's any woman I've ever met who I'd call a witch, it would be her."

Tara nodded. True, though Miss Lucy didn't look anything like a stereotypical witch with warts and a long nose, she still had a powerful aura that dispelled fools and weaklings.

"What else?" Tara asked. It couldn't have just been meeting Miss Lucy that made Richard think that Tara could perform magic.

"Next, you made tea for me. When we were dating. When I caught a cold."

Tara thought about it for a moment. She vaguely remembered him being sick once. She'd made tea for him other times as well, though. "What was magical about the tea I made?"

Richard sat and thought for a moment, his lips pressed together in a hard line. "I've never, *never*, had anything herbal or pharmaceutical that actually worked on one of my colds. But that tea basically cured me overnight."

"You might have had just a mild cold," Tara said. What had she put into it? She didn't remember.

"No," Richard said. "Every fall, since I was a kid, I'd catch a cold. I knew what its course was. I would turn into a snot factory for six days, then it would slowly taper off. But I wouldn't be well for ten days at a minimum. After drinking your tea, I was back on my feet after three. That had never happened to me before. Not ever."

"Okay," Tara said. "But why did you consider that magic? It might have been just the right herbs for you. No magic involved."

"Because I'd hoarded some of that batch, planning to use it the next year. However, it didn't work."

Before Tara could point out that maybe it was just the herbs had gone stale, Richard continued. "We weren't dating by that point, but you agreed to make me more tea. I watched you mix it up. The herbs jumped into your hand when you reached for them."

Tara frowned. She didn't think that actually happened. "You were sick," she said slowly. "Maybe you had a fever."

"That's what I thought at first. However, since we were no longer dating, you let me watch you more often. You were never in doubt about what to use because the herbs gave themselves to you. It was kinda freaky, but also, awesome."

"Huh," Tara said. She'd have to watch herself more carefully the next time she made a sachet or even tea. It wouldn't do for just anyone to look at her and know that she was a witch.

"So, was that it?" Richard asked with a cocky grin. "Was it national 'witch coming out day' or something?"

Tara sighed and shook her head. "I wish that was it. But I actually have a very serious question for you. You remember the research you did for me about London Bridges, last year?"

Richard instantly sobered. "I do. And the supposition that women died, or committed suicide, every time one of the bridges of Portland were either built or had major repair work done."

"There's a supernatural creature who binds the heart of a witch to the base of every bridge," Tara admitted.

"Really?" Richard said, his eyes taking on a certain intensity that Tara recognized from early in their relationship: She'd just awoken the research librarian, given him a mystery to unravel.

Woe to the ignorant.

"He's called the Riprap man," Tara said.

"Riprap—named after the boulders at the base of the footings of a bridge?" Richard guessed.

Tara nodded. "Yes. He sacrifices witches to the spirit of the river, supposedly so that the river won't destroy the bridge during the next flood."

"Ohhh," Richard said.

Tara could already see him forming his search parameters in order to investigate more.

A cold wet wind blew across the restaurant. Tara held up her hand before Richard could say anything more.

Cautiously, Tara looked around.

The Riprap man stared at her hungrily from across the now mostly empty room. He wore his human aspect, looking like an old-fashioned gentleman from the 1900s, with a brown wool vest, suit jacket, and pants. A black string tie was knotted around the collar of a brilliantly white shirt. He still had a bowler hat, though it was pushed back further onto the back of his head.

For the first time, the Riprap man's face appeared clear. He had pasty white skin and green eyes, a round face with high cheekbones, giving him more of a boyish look. His neck and chin were shaved clean of what probably would have been a sandy-blond beard.

He was disappointingly ordinary looking. Without the old-fashioned clothing, Tara wouldn't have given him a second look. And as it was one of the hipper parts of Portland, most of the other people in the neighborhood wouldn't notice him either.

The smell of wet ropes washed over Tara, overtaking the homey smells of frying meat and potatoes. She suddenly gulped at the air, feeling as though it had grown heavy with moisture, making it difficult to breathe.

Defiantly, Tara called up a light breeze around her, which allowed her to breathe more easily.

The Riprap man merely smiled at her, a cruel, predatory smile. The smile of a man certain that his target would never be able to escape.

Then he looked down.

Soot suddenly stood beside him, looking up at him warily.

The Riprap man reached out and petted the dog's head as if it were the most natural thing in the world.

Without giving Tara another look, the Riprap man turned and headed for the door.

Soot stayed right at his heels.

Tara whistled abruptly, hoping that Soot would hear her, that whatever spell the Riprap man had cast on the wind would break easily.

Both the dog and the man disappeared before they reached the door.

Tara shuddered. Did the Riprap man now have her tamed wind? Was he going to turn Soot against Tara? She had no idea.

"What just happened?" Richard asked quietly. "You were watching something I couldn't see."

Tara gulped again. "That was the Riprap man. I think…I think he has my wind."

"Huh?" Richard said, looking confused.

Tara couldn't help but smile. Finally, something Richard didn't know about.

Tara explained all that had happened, how she'd had to fight the Riprap man during the solstice, how she'd made a bargain with the spirit of the river, and then more recently, how there was more than one school of witchcraft and she was actually more of a hedgewitch. And she'd appeared to have tamed a wind that appeared mostly as a black greyhound.

"What herbs do you use to call a greyhound?" Richard asked.

"I didn't…Hmmm," Tara said, thinking. She hadn't approached the question that way. Kyle had initially gathered wind to him using "schooled" magic, as it were. Could she use a similar spell to bring Soot back?

"Thank you," Tara said after a moment. She paused and gulped again. "This is why I want to invite you to be an honorary member of my coven."

Richard sat up straighter but didn't say anything. She could tell he was thinking furiously about it.

"It may be dangerous for you, because of the Riprap man. And I don't know if you could ever be a full member, because you don't have any magic." Tara had checked more than once, but Richard had never appeared to notice the back room of Ye Olde Magick Shoppe.

"What would you want me to do?" Richard asked.

"What you do naturally," Tara said. "Since I'm starting my own coven, I don't have access to any of the ancient books of witch lore. And I have no idea what my powers might be as a hedgewitch. Any and all information you can bring would be greatly appreciated."

"I'd do that because we were friends," Richard pointed out. "Why bring me into the coven?"

"Because I want you to be part of it," Tara said. She tried to find the words. "When Kyle first mentioned it, I thought he was crazy. But the more I thought about it, the more you just fit."

Richard gave her a smile and nodded. "Like the herbs. You have knowledge about what should work. But you also follow your own instincts."

"Not as much as I could have, but yeah, like that," Tara said. She did make a special blend of tea every morning, depending on how she felt, not according to any lore.

"I accept your offer," Richard said.

"Are you sure?" Tara said, wanting to verify.

Richard gave her an adamant nod. "Yes. Besides, when else am I going to be able to watch other people perform magic?"

"You know you won't be able to tell anyone about this, right?" Tara added. Maybe she should have started with that.

"I know," Richard said. "It was the main thing that drove us apart, when we first broke up." He paused, then added, "At some point, I might ask for dispensation to tell Jeannie. I wouldn't right now, though. Not until I figure out if she's actually the woman I want to marry."

"Really?" Tara asked, surprised. Richard had always proclaimed that he wasn't the marrying type. He'd only been dating Jeannie a few months.

Richard shrugged. "We'll see. We're starting to talk about moving in together. But I don't know."

"Wow," Tara said, impressed. "I just want you to be happy," she added, despite feeling a slight tinge of envy. Not that she wanted to marry Richard, but it had been so long since she'd had someone in her life. Besides, Richard had been a dear friend to her for years. She honestly did want the best for him.

"I have a question," Richard said after a moment. "Are you looking to recruit other witches for your coven?"

"I am," Tara said. "What, do you know any?"

Though she'd never thought about it, it really wouldn't surprise her if he did.

"Maybe. Maybe not. I can't tell, not for certain," Richard said, hesitating. "But if there's anyone who I've ever met who's possibly magical, it would be Kaede."

"Ka-ee-dee?" Tara asked, carefully pronouncing the name.

"Yes," Richard said. "Ze runs Hallowed Ground, a shelter up in the Lloyd district, off Weidler."

Tara blinked, surprised that Richard was that familiar with alternate pronouns. The name didn't give any hint of a gender either.

"You should go down tomorrow and volunteer," Richard told her firmly. "It's a good place, and ze could always use another hand."

"All right," Tara said slowly. What else did she have to do on a Sunday afternoon? Except to try to free Soot from the Riprap man.

Richard agreed to meet with Tara, Ginny, and Kyle on Monday night before the pair of them headed out the door.

To Tara's surprise, Soot sat just outside the door, waiting for Tara. He came bounding up, still part puppy, dancing around her, happy to see her.

She introduced him to Richard with the instruction, "Know his scent."

Richard held out his hand and let the dog sniff at it. Though greyhounds were more sight than nose dogs, Tara figured that Soot would be able to do both. After saying goodnight, Tara stood for a moment, staring at Soot.

Was the wind hers again? Had that whistle broken the hold the Riprap man had had? Or would the Riprap man be able to call Soot to him at any time?

Tara didn't know, and she didn't think Ginny would know either.

And Soot wasn't telling.

SUNDAY MORNING BROUGHT MORE RAIN. TARA WAS actually happy to hear it pattering against her window as she slowly came awake. It was a welcome respite from the long hot summer. She still took her tea outside to the balcony to drink it, even if she didn't sit on one of the wet metal chairs, but rather stared out over the small courtyard at the buildings just across the way.

Maybe the next place she moved to, she'd have a better balcony, one she could sit on most of the year.

First she'd have to find a job. It was time for her to move on from everything. She had a shift Tuesday morning at Ye Olde Magick Shoppe, as the shop owner Patricia had extra work to do before the equinox on Wednesday.

But that was Tara's last shift, as far as she knew. Patricia would probably never call her back, too afraid of the "bad luck" Tara supposedly carried with her as a victim of the Riprap man.

However, Tara was forming her own coven. It felt good, but odd.

After enjoying a second cup of tea, Tara finally felt ready to face the world. Soot wasn't around that morning. Maybe he'd been chased off by the rain. Tara didn't feel as antsy that morning either, not as she had Saturday morning.

Had that been part of her connection to Soot? Was it now broken?

Tara gave a sharp whistle, and was relieved when Soot popped up on the balcony almost immediately. "Good boy," Tara said, patting his sleek head. "Follow me today, okay?" she asked him.

Soot cocked his head to one side as if he didn't understand. Tara imagined herself walking along the sidewalk with Soot at her heels, on her way to the train.

Soot cocked his head to the other side, as if considering her request. Then he disappeared again.

Fine. She couldn't rely on him if she needed help. Message received.

Though she wasn't sure why she was feeling so hesitant. Kaede wouldn't attack her, would ze? Richard would only admit to having met Kaede at a volunteer event at the library. He still couldn't say why he thought ze was a witch. But he was adamant that ze might be.

As Tara walked down the street toward the MAX station, a cold wind nipped at her ankles. She turned around to see that Soot was there. He'd taken her command literally, and had done just exactly as she'd asked.

No more, no less.

Tara was going to have to read some dog training books.

Still, she praised Soot for following her, and imagined him there when she got off the MAX train.

Luckily, the Riprap man didn't appear on the train, as he had before. Still, she couldn't help but think about him and wonder when he'd make his next attack.

Downtown was still pretty quiet that early on a Sunday. Tara had checked the website for Hallowed Ground and found that while the general doors opened at noon, volunteers were expected to arrive by nine.

There was already a line at the front door by the time Tara arrived. Mainly chronic homeless people, with huge shopping carts piled high with all their personal belongings. A few street kids hung out as well, strumming a guitar.

Surprisingly, none of them bothered Tara as she walked by. Instead, one of the old women with only a few teeth left in her crinkly apple face pointed to the side of the building and said, "Volunteer entrance is that way."

"Thank you," Tara said.

Tara passed by the front of the building. It looked like converted office space, with a door in the center and large windows on either side. Cream-colored drapes hid the inside from the curious. Above the main floor, it looked as though there were three stories of apartments. All the windows were lined with aluminum foil to keep out the western sun.

Tara made her way along the side of the building and to the back. A large, hand-painted sign above the door said, "Volunteers only. Yes, that means you."

Cautiously, Tara stuck her head in the door. It opened onto a long hallway. She heard the banging of pots to her right, and either tables or chairs scraping against a floor straight ahead of her.

Taking a deep breath, Tara stepped across the threshold.

For a moment, she paused. She had a feeling of *something* present. It was similar to the feeling she'd gotten when she entered the garden that had held the meditation maze that the witches had used for passing within. It wasn't the same, however. This space wasn't as watchful.

It was still a *separate* space. Maybe not sacred, not as she understood it, but not completely mundane either.

Maybe Richard had been right.

Tara walked directly into the kitchen. It was a large open area, maybe thirty feet square, going up at least two stories. Industrial ovens, stoves, and grills lined the walls, most of them unmanned. A huge dishwasher stood in the corner, where large racks of dishes would be pushed through and sanitized.

In the center of the room, the volunteers had gathered around a series of tables, all chatting and chopping vegetables. Tara recognized the rhythm of people who had worked together for a long while— mostly women, but a few men as well.

A young woman came in from behind Tara, carrying a large basket of potatoes. "Can I help you?" she asked as she walked past Tara, delivering her goods to the table. She wore an artfully torn white T-shirt that showed off her black bra, along with jeans that were also torn deliberately instead of through use. Her blonde hair came straight out of a bottle, and she had the modern day armor of piercings scattered across her face, up both her ears, as well as in her collarbone.

Though the woman had a level of toughness to her, she was bird-thin and brittle. Tara felt as though she'd break this woman in two if she wasn't careful, even though they were roughly the same height.

"I'm here to volunteer," Tara said, keeping her smile friendly and non-threatening.

"Good! Good," the woman said. She returned Tara's bright smile, her pale blue eyes taking on an additional warmth. "Welcome to Hallowed Ground. This is your first time, yes?"

"It is," Tara said, nodding. She added, "I'm comfortable helping wherever you need hands."

The woman paused and looked at Tara more closely. "Ah," she said after a moment. "You need to talk to Kaede first."

"All right," Tara said. Had this woman just figured out Tara was a witch? Or was there something else about her?

"Ze is out front, setting the lines," the woman said. "I'm Alaska, by the way."

"Tara," she said, nodding.

Out front turned out to be about three times as large as the kitchen area. Tara had assumed that "setting the lines" had meant setting up some sort of rope line, in order to direct people. Instead, all the tables had been pushed to the edges of room, with the chairs piled up haphazardly on top, and would fall if someone wasn't careful getting them down.

The only person in the room—Kaede, Tara

presumed—knelt on the ground in the center of the space and drew lines in chalk on the wooden floor.

A pentagram, Tara realized as she drew closer.

Kaede was chanting one of the hymns that Tara knew. As Tara didn't want to disturb the blessing taking place, bringing the warmth of the hearth into a new home, she joined along with the hymn instead, quietly adding her voice and her power.

Richard had been correct. Kaede was a witch, and a high-powered one at that. The strength of zir blessing flowed out to all the corners of the room, traveling up the walls and seeping into the building itself. Would Tara now feel the space as more sacred, if she'd entered after Kaede had finished zir hymn?

Tara stayed where she was, outside the pentagram, as Kaede finished. Ze looked Asian to Tara, Japanese, if she had to guess. Kaede wore zir hair shaved short, so it was just black fuzz across zir scalp. Ze had on a red T-shirt with white lettering, the name of some band Tara thought looked vaguely familiar, with capri jeans showing off muscled calves and bare feet. Ze didn't have any piercings or visible tattoos, which surprised Tara.

When Kaede finished the last line of the pentagram, timed with the last line of the hymn, ze stood up and frankly appraised Tara. "Alaska sent you out, didn't she?" Zir voice didn't give any indication of gender either.

Tara found herself curious, though she knew it was none of her business.

"She did," Tara said, nodding.

"Figured," Kaede said. "She assumed the little rich white girl would get freaked out by the pentagram."

Tara shrugged. "She was wrong." Though she probably did look like a "little rich white girl."

"That's Alaska's main problem. She always misjudges people. Both the good as well as the bad," Kaede said, shaking zir head. "So why are you here, Miss Witch?" Kaede leaned back and folded zir arms across zir chest.

"My name's Tara. And I did plan on volunteering for the day," Tara said. She didn't like how she was having to prove herself to these people.

Then again, it was their territory that she'd come into.

"And?" Kaede said, challenging.

Tara tilted her head to the side. She didn't want to invite Kaede into the coven if she didn't think they could work together. And she hadn't been in the other person's presence long enough to make that call yet, either.

"I don't know what 'and' is, or even if there is an 'and,'" Tara confessed. "There might be. But I don't know. Not yet."

Kaede nodded. "Got a story, don't you, Tara. That's okay. Most of the folks here have stories, and none of them are sweet. All right. We can talk after we get everyone fed and settled. Let's get this place ready."

Tara followed Kaede, as that seemed to be what the person wanted, carefully pulling down chairs and setting up tables. At least Tara was stronger than she looked, keeping herself in shape with swimming and yoga, so she was easily able to keep up with Kaede.

"Hallowed Ground came from the idea that the neighborhood has to take care of itself," Kaede told Tara. "There are no good corporations. Each and every one of them has blood on their hands. The only way you can achieve a working society is if everyone contributes according to their abilities, and only takes according to their need."

"Communist?" Tara couldn't help but ask, recognizing the quote as coming from Lenin.

Kaede rolled zir eyes. "The communist society, the worker's paradise, was doomed from the start. It was too large of an organization. You can't run a country that way. You have to start small. Dig deep roots and grow out from there."

"I see," Tara said, though she wasn't certain that she did. Covens tended to exist in their own sort of space as well, but it wasn't the same. The only members of their community were witches.

"We got more than a soup kitchen, here," Kaede said. "Will give you a tour later if you decide to stick around. Rooms upstairs to give people a way to transition off the street. After-school programs for kids. Mediation nights for people to solve their disputes. Regular education about government services."

Tara was curious about that. "Mediation? Education?"

"You know the best way to decrease the homeless population? Not to focus on housing everyone, but instead, to focus on prevention," Kaede said. "The number of people forced out into the street keeps rising along with housing prices. Every person you place gets replaced with someone else out on the street in less than three months. If you don't have as many people being forced out, you can actually decrease the number living out there."

"That's kind of brilliant," Tara said. She helped Kaede lift down another table, setting it into place. "Do you work with a coven?" She had to ask, though she suspected she already knew the answer.

"Don't talk to me about those stuck-up witches," Kaede said, anger deepening zir voice. "They only want to help their own. They wouldn't even contemplate bringing in a mundane."

"Ah," Tara said, nodding. That made sense. It was one of the reasons why she'd been so uncomfortable with Miss Lucy. The entire coven had just struck her as selfish, only wanting their own members to prosper. That, plus the fact that they cursed people, bringing them harm without a good reason, at least as far as Tara was concerned.

"What, you forming a coven?" Kaede asked, zir dark brown eyes peering intently at Tara.

"I am," Tara admitted. "And I have already invited a mundane to come and be an honorary member."

"What?" Kaede said. "Okay, Tara, you got my attention now. Why a mundane?"

"He's a research librarian. I don't have access to any books or ancient lore. He already had guessed that I was a witch, so he volunteered to help."

"Interesting," Kaede said.

"He was actually the one who recommended that I come to see you," Tara said.

Kaede picked up a few chairs and started hauling them to tables. Tara followed suit.

"I take it something happened with your old coven," Kaede said.

"Yes. And that's part of why I'm not sure there's an 'and' here," Tara said, referring to earlier in their conversation. "There's a creature haunting me. I don't want to bring danger to you or your community."

Kaede just nodded. "The people with the most need are the ones who show up at my door," ze said plainly. "The fact that you're here probably means you need to be here. We'll talk, more, after service."

"Thank you," Tara said. She wasn't sure what else to say. Hallowed Ground felt just like that to her, a sacred space, now that she'd been there for a short while. A place where possibly she could belong, if she was accepted.

After they finished setting up the long tables and chairs, as well as the tables around the edges for serving food, Kaede sent Tara back to the kitchen to help there. Tara chopped vegetables and helped prepare a simple meal for their service. While some of the herbs were fresh, most of the seasoning came in industrial-sized shakers. Tara took over one of the potato dishes, making sure that it was as tasty as possible, given the constraints.

At one point, an older Japanese woman came shuffling into the kitchen. She wore a beautiful peach-colored kimono with a pattern of lucky clouds floating across. Her black obi was tied tightly around her tiny waist, the folds perfectly pressed. White tabi socks stuck out under the kimono, along with old-fashioned bamboo and wooden sandals.

She regally nodded to Alaska and some of the other people in the room before starting the process of making a huge batch of barley tea.

When Kaede came into the room, ze just shook zir head at the old woman. "What are you doing here?"

The older woman replied in what Tara assumed was Japanese. Kaede said something in reply in that language. It quickly escalated into an argument, with the pair of them soon shouting at one another. Tara wondered if Kaede was telling the old woman to go home. But the woman flat refused, and instead serenely turned back to her tea as if nothing had happened.

Alaska came over to Tara and spoke quietly in her ear. "That's Kaede's grandmother. She comes by every day we serve to make tea. In proper robes."

"Okay," Tara said, confused. But then again, families were weird.

Just before service, Kaede called everyone together and had them join hands in a circle. Ze prayed for a moment, asking for Brigit's blessings, before releasing them to do the best they could that day.

Then the doors opened, and chaos ensued.

CHAPTER 5

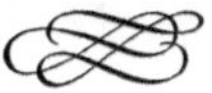

Hedgewitches have turned out to be wily opponents. Of course they still lose, in the end. But I believe that, because a hedgewitch is on her own, she has developed more survival skills. I have switched back to hunting the schooled witches to do my mighty task, made more difficult by the rate of progress throughout the entire glorious city of Portland. The river god does not see the opportunities that I do; however, he does recognize the necessity to prolong the life of his most ardent follower. I shall have to travel back to the heartwaters of the river again. This time it won't be as arduous a task. Roads multiply like locusts. Rail lines choke the wilderness. The people grow soft in such decadence. Still, I have my sworn duty, and the river god's floods are just spats. Nothing mighty enough to wash away the city, though sometimes I'm tempted to direct His mighty wrath to do just that.

Wilson Evermore, Aging Magician and Weary Traveler,
1925

TARA WASN'T sure that she'd ever been so tired before, at least, not like this.

On the one hand, she liked people, and she'd honestly missed working at the shop, dealing with crowds.

However, this was something very different. She'd been a runner during the meal, as she was new and the community didn't really know her. So Tara had hauled pots of soup and potatoes, along with baskets of bread, from the kitchen to the serving tables.

Many, if not all, of the people who'd come to the soup kitchen line had brought something to donate, whether it be a pair of clean socks that they'd acquired and felt as though they could pass along, slightly worn shoes, clean-ish blankets, or food they'd received at a different food bank that they hadn't liked.

Tara had ended up carrying those into the kitchen as well, prepping the food so it could be shared, then bringing it back out and serving it. She'd also learned where the laundry room and supply room were, starting up a load so that the bounty that had been brought in could be redistributed among the community.

Though Tara had never worked in a soup kitchen before, she didn't think that this was the way one would normally be run. The homeless were just that—homeless. However, here the expectation appeared to be that they were to contribute what they could, when they could.

These people may have been sleeping out on the street, but they *belonged* to this place in a way that made Tara's heart ache.

It occurred to her that she wasn't the rich one here, not by a long shot. She did have a few good friends. However, even she had to admit that her covens had never been actual communities. Not like the people here.

They looked out for each other. Tara watched the more able fill trays and plates of food for those in wheelchairs, or who hobbled on canes.

Though Tara had never been so involved with any of the homeless before, there was only one person who frightened her. He was rambling about the government wiring his body together wrong, asking how much poison was in the bread, comparing the water to a river of piss.

He was so obviously insane that he struck Tara as an alien, barely human anymore.

One of the servers was familiar with him, and told Tara that he was a schizophrenic, off his meds, and unfortunately, high on something. Kaede took the young man out of the line and to the side, trying to get him to stop shaking. Ze made sure that he ate at least some of what was on his plate before issuing him back outside. He wasn't part of the community here, and he was too high—possibly a danger not only to himself but to others. One of the other regulars volunteered to go sit with him until he was able to take care of himself again.

After the food rush had passed, and everyone had eaten at the long communal tables, many stayed where they were, chatting with their neighbors. Tara thought she saw a bottle of wine being passed between one group, but no one else seemed to care.

The stately grandmother in her beautiful obi came out and served tea to everyone who wanted it. She moved with incredible grace in her wooden sandals, treating each person with a reserved dignity. It was like a moving ballet. Tara didn't understand why it was so important, but it seemed to her to be the final prayer in a circle, the blessing that all sought.

Tara wished that she could help, that she had something more to give to these people. They needed hands to help, of course. But she didn't have money she could give them. There had to be something she could do.

Kids soon broke out their school books. More than one of the older clients sat with them, helping them with their homework, listening as the kids talked. In one corner, one of the older men sat with a couple of very young children and told them stories.

Tara spent her time cleaning up, carrying away the very few remaining plates and used utensils—most of the people had bussed themselves. She also was pointed to a couple of pitchers of water, and delivered that to people still sitting around. She was debating where she was needed next. Only so many people could work running the sanitizer in the kitchen, too many bodies got in the way there.

It wasn't until she heard one of the kids complaining about being so stressed it was giving him headaches that she saw opportunity knocking.

"Tell me about your headaches," she said, drawing slowly toward the group. "Do they start in your neck? Or in your forehead."

"Back of my skull," the boy admitted quietly. He wore a white thermal-underwear shirt under a blue-and-white checked flannel shirt. His skin looked too pale, and his gray-green eyes stood out huge in his face. Dirty blond hair stuck up all over his head.

"I may have something for you," Tara said, getting an idea.

She rushed back to the kitchen. It was empty. The latest round of dishes were drying and the helpers had left. Tara reached for the cheap English Breakfast tea that she'd seen on one of the shelves. She tore off the string tying the folded teabag together, grabbed a bowl, then dumped the leaves (more like tea dust and twigs) out. Then she chopped up some of the mint she'd found, a pinch of dried ginger, and for luck, just a dash of cayenne, all the while humming a soothing melody.

After she retied the string around the ends of the folded teabag, she walked back out to the front room. "It isn't much," she said, handing the young man a single teabag. "But it should help calm your nerves, help you focus more. You need to get some hot water in a cup, put the tea bag in there for five minutes to steep, then gently squeeze it out. You may be able to get two cups from that."

"Wow, gee, thanks," the boy said, a little confused.

"Kaede sometimes makes sachets for people," one of the nearby girls said. "You make those too?"

Tara's fingers automatically found the sachet that

she always carried with her, one for courage and protection. "You can have mine," she said.

The girl made a face at the faded pink bag.

Tara saw her mistake. "Though I should probably remix it for you. What do you need it for?"

The smile that lit up the girl's face warmed Tara through to her toes. "I got brothers," she said.

"Oh?" Tara asked, trying to be nonchalant but hoping that she wasn't about to hear a tale of abuse.

"They won't come here. They do stupid things, and are in a gang. You got something to help with that?" the girl said.

"They don't need courage," Tara said slowly. "Or protection. They need belonging."

"Yes! Exactly. I can't get 'em here," the girl said. "Where they might stand a chance."

What would promote being together? Sticky plants, like ivy and honeysuckle, Tara decided. And though Marshmallow wasn't like the actual food, maybe that too. "I can bring you something tomorrow," she said slowly.

"Great! I'll stop by after school, as usual, to do my homework," the girl said. "I'm Kaneshia, by the way. And that goof is Eric."

"Tara," she said, introducing herself.

It surprised her how the young people drew her into their conversation. It wasn't because she belonged there, she knew that.

It took her a while to realize that mainly, these young teens (thirteen and fourteen) really just wanted her to listen. None of the adults in their lives would. It was a huge draw for Hallowed Ground. The older people there considered it their job to listen, really listen, to these youth.

By the time Kaede came to find Tara, she knew that she would be returning regularly, whether Kaede became a member of Tara's fledgling coven or not.

Tara might have found a place where she could belong.

KAEDE TOOK TARA BACK TOWARD THE DOOR SHE'D entered into the building, to a small side office off the main hallway. Now that Tara took a closer look, she saw that white chalk lines had been drawn on the white paint. They were barely visible unless she stared at them, and then they made the hairs on the back of Tara's neck stand up. They reminded her of designs Miss Lucy had used for protection, the kind of spell that promised pain to any who trespassed.

"I used to try to put sachets on the door, or above the door frame," Kaede said, indicating the lines of protection. "But too many people stole them, seeking something to help protect them out on the street." Ze shrugged and opened the door. "I don't blame them. So I had to come up with something to get them to respect this doorway and this office."

"Why?" Tara asked, stepping into the crowded space. The room was tiny, maybe six by six. A large gray filing cabinet loomed in one corner, papers piled up on top. A long desk jutted out from the wall. Papers piled up on it as well. To Tara it looked like organized chaos, as the stacks were all neat. The room smelled of the food they'd cooked in the kitchen, with an underlying dark scent of barley tea.

Kaede slid behind the desk and plopped zirself down in the old office chair there, while gesturing for Tara to take one of the two mismatched chairs on the other side of the desk.

"They need to respect someone else's space," Kaede said seriously. "They're out on the street and used to trespassing, considering everything theirs. As part of relearning to be in society, and being part of a community, they need this sort of boundary, though there's nothing here for anyone to see or steal."

Tara wondered about that. The room did appear to mostly contain paperwork. An ancient computer monitor sat on one corner of the desk, with an equally antiquated keyboard, both connected to an out–of-sight computer that was probably out of date as well. The desk lamp had seen better days. Dust covered the light-colored shade and the porcelain base appeared to be held together with duct tape.

"I like it here, at Hallowed Ground," Tara said. "I'd like to come back and volunteer, regardless of your decision about joining my coven."

That earned Tara a huge smile from Kaede. "I'd wondered. You seemed to fit, which, believe me, not all the volunteers who come through here do. So tell me about this coven of yours, and why you need another witch."

Tara told Kaede everything, from her own training starting with Miss Lucy, to Sheila, to being haunted by the Riprap man. Then she talked about Ginny, and how she was probably a hedgewitch herself, as well as about Richard and Kyle.

"What would you like to do here?" Kaede asked after a moment. "If you came back to volunteer?"

Tara explained about making the tea for the teen who was so stressed about everything, as well as making a sachet for the girl's brothers, to try to bring the family together.

Kaede sat nodding after Tara finished, a comfortable silence filling the small office. "I'm good with spaces," Kaede said after a few moments. "I'm a schooled witch, made it to the fifth circle, circle of water."

Tara sat up straighter, surprised. Kaede didn't appear to be that old. How powerful was ze?

"I started young," Kaede explained. "Grandmother made sure of that."

Given Kaede's sour expression, Tara had no doubt as to whom Kaede referred to, the older woman who'd served tea that afternoon.

"But I hated their structure, their strict rules," Kaede said. "They didn't fit me. Not the me I was discovering, the being that is neither male nor female, the inclusive one. I'd already started volunteering here, at Hallowed Ground. Discovered my true calling as an anarchist."

Tara saw much more research in her future. She'd

thought that anarchists just tore things down. They didn't build communities, did they?

"Everyone should be expected to contribute to the community, not just sit at the top of the food chain and direct their human slaves," Kaede said hotly. Then ze grinned and shook zir head. "But you don't need a lecture. We'll just slowly indoctrinate you."

"Okay," Tara said, though she wasn't sure what that really meant.

"In your ideal world, what would you do?" Kaede asked.

"Open a tea shop," Tara said without pausing. She'd been thinking about that off and on for the past few days. "Not someplace that sold regular tea, or mixed blends. But a place where someone could come and get special mixes, specifically blended just for them."

Kaede smiled at her. "I was hoping you'd say that. How do you feel about working here during the week, afternoons and evenings?"

"What do you mean?" Tara asked, confused. "Like work here, like a job?"

Kaede rocked zir head back and forth. "Kind of. It wouldn't be fulltime. I can't afford that. But I have an opening for an another coordinator. Basically, it involves running the afterschool program."

"I don't have any experience doing that," Tara said. "I don't have any kids—never really wanted them." Wouldn't that type of coordinator need to have at least a degree in social work? Tara's degree was in English literature by default, not because she'd actually liked it.

"The program pretty much runs itself," Kaede

assured her. "I need someone here to open the doors and let the kids in, count noses and keep track of things. There are a few adults in the community who come and monitor the teens. The kids are pretty well behaved for the most part, just need to be reminded now and again to not be such hooligans."

"But why me?" Tara asked, still confused.

"I can give you a monthly stipend for supplies for making your teas and sachets," Kaede said. "And I'm sure that you'll be able to sweet talk some of the covens into donating supplies as well. As for 'why you,' it's because I want you to set up that tea shop. Here, in Hallowed Ground."

"You want me to do what?" Tara said, trying to keep her voice modulated and not actually yell.

Kaede grinned at her. "Make your specialty teas. And your sachets. For the kids who need them."

Ze appeared to be thinking for a moment, before ze added, "Set up a barter system with the kids. Be creative with that. It might be passing a test, or spending an hour doing homework without interruption, or even wild gardening, harvesting things you need from the city parks."

"So my customers would be the kids who came in for the afternoon program?" Tara said, starting to understand. Starting to smile.

"The ones who need it the most," Kaede said. "Some of them need real magic in their lives. A bunch of them just require an adult who listens and who tries to help."

"Wow," Tara said. "I never...I never would have

considered this." She knew her answer immediately, however. "I would love to," Tara said, though she'd never thought that working with teenagers would have excited her. "I'll still have to get another job," she warned. A part-time salary from a shelter wouldn't cover her expenses.

Who would contribute supplies for her teas? Patricia would, certainly. Sheila, or more likely, Aaloka, might, if for nothing else, to assuage their guilt. Would Miss Lucy? Or the people Tara used to babysit for?

"That's pretty much everyone's life here," Kaede said. "Those who can, work a couple of other jobs so that I don't have to pay them."

Tara nodded, hearing the expectation laid out clearly in those words. Kaede would pay her at the start, but eventually, she should figure out how to make money from something else, while still volunteering.

"As for your coven," Kaede said slowly. "I'm interested. I'd really like to see a coven run on merit as opposed to a strict hierarchy. I'm not saying that I'll be able to stay, but I'd like to help, at least short term."

"Really? That would be wonderful!" Tara said. Kaede was a powerful witch, of higher level than Kyle. Still, she had to ask, "Are you sure?"

Kaede nodded. "Yes. I understand that this Riprap man may attempt to bring bad luck to the center, to my kids. But as I said, I'm good with spaces. Let him try."

Tara had the impression of Kaede growing larger, a suit of old-fashioned Japanese armor encasing zir, bearing a katana with a glowing blade.

The Riprap man had no idea what he was about to face.

TARA FOUND HERSELF PAUSING AFTER SHE LEFT Hallowed Ground, blinking her eyes against the dim afternoon light. She'd stepped out of one world and into the next. No wonder Kaede called zirself good with spaces. The community center was sacred, separate from the rest of the mundane world. Tara felt that now, deep in her bones.

She took a deep breath.

The smell of stagnant water overwhelmed her. She coughed, gagging.

The Riprap man stood at the corner of the building. His bare torso had the appearance of stones piled together, though he still wore pants and his bowler hat.

He placed one large, granite palm on the corner of the building and shoved, just once.

The entire building groaned, the timbers creaking. Cracks formed in the stucco walls.

Crap! Was he going to push it over? Tara readied herself to rush him, see if she could physically tackle the creature.

But the building appeared to fight back. A bolt of lightning raced across the wall closest to Tara, running from the door to where the Riprap man was touching the building. He jerked his hand back, surprised.

Yes, Kaede was very good with spaces, it appeared.

The Riprap man turned to glare at Tara.

She gulped, the air suddenly thick and hard to breathe.

"What do you want?" she demanded as she tried to clear the air around her.

The message came clear, carried on waves of rage and mortification. Tara was the Riprap man's rival for the river god's affection. He intended to show the river god just how badly He'd chosen.

The eventual battle between Tara and the Riprap man would be epic. But he would prevail in the end, and the river god would see the error of His ways.

Tara snorted. "Even if you defeat me, which you won't, your river god is still going to be on the lookout for someone more sympathetic. You're not a water person. Creature. Monster. Whatever."

"No," the Riprap man said. His features wavered, and suddenly the old-fashioned gentleman who Tara had first met stood in front of her. He had a clear tenor voice that cut through the still air surrounding them. "He will cleave unto me and no other."

"You do know that sounds like you're pursuing a homosexual relationship, right?" Tara pointed out. If the Riprap man was a modern creature, she wouldn't have bothered saying anything. However, given how old the Riprap man actually was, she hoped that would bother him.

The Riprap man merely shrugged. "The meaning of the words have changed. Not the sentiment. You know nothing of devotion, of commitment. Of covenant."

Tara blinked, surprised that the Riprap man was

speaking with her, that they were having an almost normal conversation.

"How do you intend to stop me?" Tara said. She figured she may as well ask.

The Riprap man gave her a sly smile. "That would be telling."

He turned and started walking away. He gave a sharp whistle just before he turned the corner.

A dark figure appeared beside him. Was that Soot? The Riprap man vanished out of sight around the corner before Tara could tell for certain.

She hurried forward, worried.

The Riprap man was nowhere to be seen.

And though she whistled and called, Soot never returned to her.

LATER THAT EVENING, TARA AND KYLE SAT IN THE darkened living room of Kyle's condo, sipping peppermint tea sweetened with a touch of warm apple cider and cinnamon. Tara told Kyle about Kaede, pleased to have another powerful witch join her coven. She was actually getting more comfortable calling it *her* coven, though she also liked Kaede's belief that the coven actually belonged to all of them.

The night felt warm outside the sliding glass door leading to the balcony, the clouds appearing orange due to their reflections of the city streetlights. Tara had stood out on the balcony for a while after she'd returned, whistling for Soot, but the wind hadn't returned to her.

Did the Riprap man now control her wind? Would Soot ever return? Tara was starting to feel the wind's absence, as if her lungs were somehow contracted and she could no longer take a deep breath.

Kyle looked worried. He wore his weekend clothes, a soft gray sweatshirt over brown jogging pants. He'd just shaved his head for the week, and the black skin glistened with the oil he'd rubbed in. "I had always thought that familiars were just a fanciful myth. Now, I'm wondering if there's some basis in it, that the hedgewitches have animals that are connected to them."

"I was thinking the same thing," Tara said. "I've sent an email to Richard, to investigate older accounts of witch familiars. I'm not hopeful that he'll find anything useful."

"Why?" Kyle asked, peering intently at her.

"Remember? According to Ginny, what works for one hedgewitch may not work for another. And whatever does work isn't necessarily consistent."

Kyle nodded and sipped his tea, his eyes still boring into her.

"What?" Tara finally asked. "You've been watching me all night." She tried to keep her tone light and not accusatory, but her worry about Soot nagged at her.

"I've never met a hedgewitch," Kyle said slowly. "But it seems to me that having so much power left unchecked is a disaster waiting to happen."

Tara blinked, surprised. "Go on," she said when he stopped talking.

"You left Miss Lucy because her magic was inwardly focused," Kyle explained. "You've said it yourself—Miss Lucy was selfish. But a hedgewitch is the same way. All that magic is just for yourself and your gain. Hedgewitches don't normally join or form covens."

"That doesn't mean that I've suddenly grown selfish," Tara pointed out. "I'm trying to create a coven, a community." His words stung more than she'd like to admit. Since leaving Hallowed Ground that afternoon, Tara had been thinking about where she fit, what it meant to have a community, to not rely on just herself so much.

"I know you believe that," Kyle said gently. "But think back to when we were at the Saturday market yesterday. You and Ginny turned people away, left and right, out of your path, without thinking about it. Your magic just did it for you."

"True," Tara said. It had surprised her how much her and Ginny's magic had cleared the path ahead of them, without either of them actually casting any spells or drinking any potions.

"Human nature is inherently selfish," Kyle continued, building his argument like the lawyer he was. "I don't believe that you would consciously use your magic for selfish gains. Unconsciously, though? When it's just a part of you?"

Tara had no answer for Kyle or his concerns. "I don't know," Tara replied after a bit. "I can try to be more conscious of it, when the magic just happens." She took a deep breath. "But as you said, this is new to both of us. I'm going to have to rely on you to be my conscience sometimes, bring things up if I don't notice."

Kyle gave her a grin. "You've been my evil conscience before, reminding me that there was more to life than just work. Now, to return the favor, I need to be your good conscience?"

Tara nodded and gave him a heartfelt smile. "Yeah. Thank you," she said.

"You're welcome," Kyle said, sipping his tea for a moment. He nodded, as if he'd come to a decision himself. "I may have another recruit for your coven. He is a being of power. He may have some human blood in him—I've never asked."

"Okay," Tara said, surprised. Though she'd known that there were beings of power, she'd never met one, or even really been taught about them. "Why would he be interested in joining my coven?"

"Honestly, he first expressed interest in you when you survived the Riprap man," Kyle said. "When I mentioned that the Riprap man had returned and you were forming your own coven as protection, he said, and I quote, 'Do keep me in mind for your little group.'" Kyle shrugged. "He's ancient. Came to the New World 'on a lark.' He's…uhm, alien."

Tara was surprised at the shudder Kyle gave. This being truly upset Kyle at a fundamental level, whether he realized it or not.

"How did you meet?" Tara asked after Kyle had taken a few deep breaths in order to recover his equilibrium.

Kyle smiled and rolled his eyes at her. "On a dating site, if you can believe it."

"What?" Tara said, completely surprised. "So you… dated? Are dating?"

"It's complicated," Kyle said. "He isn't human," he reiterated. "He has different needs. And he helped heal me and my psychic injuries more than anyone else. When he makes an effort, he's not that disturbing."

"Okay," Tara said, not sure what else to say. "What's his name?"

Kyle shook his head. "Lucius. That isn't his real name, though. He told me he took it after that wizard in the Harry Potter movies."

Tara blinked, surprised. "Why would he do that? Why would he take a name like that?"

"You'll see," Kyle said. "If you're game, you can meet him tomorrow at one P.M."

Tara paused, her mouth open. A part of her wanted to say, "Of course, I'll meet with him." Another part of her, however, was cautious, particularly in light of Kyle's misgivings about her power.

"I will meet with him," Tara said slowly. "But I will not guarantee that he has a place in the coven."

"Good," Kyle said. "That was exactly what your conscience was hoping you'd say. He represents a lot of power. But like your own hedgewitch magic, he's impossible to control. I would call him selfish. However, he would deny that. He has strict morals. They just aren't necessarily the same as yours or mine."

"I'll keep that in mind," Tara assured him. The other beings, the elders, those with power, were the basis of many human myths. However, as individuals, they were both more as well as less than the stories made them to be.

Who was it who had described elves as brilliant and perilous? Not that Lucius was necessarily an elf, though he might be considerably more dangerous than anyone Tara had ever met before.

Kyle smiled and relaxed. Tara suddenly realized it was the first time that he'd relaxed all evening, that he'd been tense, anticipating this conversation.

Was it because Kyle didn't trust Tara?

Or was it because he didn't trust Lucius?

CHAPTER 6

The journey to the headwaters of the mighty Willamette took more than a year the first time I went. This time, it took merely three months. The end of my pilgrimage was the most difficult, going up mountain trails. My magic sustained me throughout. This wilderness sings to my heart. I am no painter or poet, however. Mere brushstrokes or words cannot capture the beauty of the mountains, the rocks and bones of the earth. I feel more youthful in this location. I assume that's because the waters are so fresh and new, though sometimes I wonder. It's as if the very earth itself supports me here. I have started to purify myself for the upcoming ceremony. The river god Mulinohana has only spoken to me once since I arrived, warning that the transformation may be painful. He assured me that I would become a better servant, as my life will be much extended. I welcome the trials that face me. Though the city of Portland

will never know my name, or how I have protected
Her, it is worth it, just to see her grow.

Wilson Evermore, Master Magician and Explorer, 1926

TARA COULDN'T HELP but feel nervous waiting for the mysterious Lucius. They were meeting at a coffee house in the Pearl District. The building was a converted warehouse, now divided up into a series of small stores. Huge wooden timbers held up the soaring ceiling. Old exposed brick made up the two outside walls, the mortar squished out like hard frosting. Only the floor was new: poured gray concrete that had been polished until it was shiny and slick.

After getting a bitter English Breakfast tea from the counter in the corner, Tara sat at one of the hard metal tables and equally cold metal chairs. As she looked around, she noticed that black and white photos hung between the windows, showing old Portland.

The photo closest to Tara's table fascinated her. It was of an old fire brigade boat pumping water at a flaming building. The fire was on the top floor of what looked like a fancy storefront. She couldn't make out the lettering that followed the curve of the façade, but the date underneath it appeared to be 1880. Smoke flew up from where the water and fire met, hazing the background.

It had taken her a few moments to realize that this photo had actually been taken during one of the huge floods. She'd originally assumed that the building that was on fire had been built next to the water. On closer examination, she realized that wasn't the case. The fire brigade boat floated in front of windows that were half submerged by the flood waters.

Was the fire on the second story of the building? The third? Tara couldn't tell. But it spoke of the desperate flooding that had occurred in Portland before humans had altered the course of the Willamette river, straightening it out as well as damming it.

"I was there. At that flood," came a deep, rich voice, a sort of "late night jazz" voice that sent cascades of goosebumps across Tara's shoulders. The voice had a slight British accent, something that Tara associated with "very posh," as it were.

"Really? You were?" Tara asked as she turned to greet Lucius.

A tall man stood next to her table, over six foot and wiry. He had thick silver hair that hung down past his shoulders. It was starting to recede from his forehead, making his face look long and thin. Brilliant blue eyes peered at her, pinning her in place. His thin lips curved in a sensuous smile, as if he liked what he saw. He had a slight cleft in his solid chin and an oversized nose, but all the parts fit together, giving him the appearance of a serious, intense older gentleman. His dark blue button-down shirt contributed to the effect.

"Yes, *really*," Lucius said, rolling his eyes at her. "Why you young people couldn't have come up with a better interrogator, I just don't know."

Tara bit her lips together so that she wouldn't end up grinning at the affronted man. "You must be Lucius," she said, rising from her table. "I'm Tara." She didn't reach out to shake his hand—Kyle had warned her that Lucius didn't enjoy casual touching any more than he did.

Lucius nodded his head to her. "Charmed, I'm sure." He glanced down at the table. "How's the tea here?"

Tara grimaced. "Not that great," she admitted.

"Coffee it is, then," Lucius said, turning abruptly and going to the counter to get his own beverage.

Tara understood why Lucius had chosen that name —he greatly resembled the character from the movie, especially given his long silver hair. He also held himself in a very stiff manner, as if he was uncomfortable in his skin.

Was that his natural appearance? Tara wasn't sure, and Kyle sure wasn't telling.

When Lucius came back, he sat without a word. He had a large mug of what looked like plain black coffee. Then he picked up a bare spoon and put it into the mug. As he stirred, a golden trail followed the path of the spoon.

"Honey," Lucius said when she looked back up at his face. "The real kind, not that fake sticky substance that they generally serve that's mostly made from corn syrup."

Tara wasn't about to point out that this place probably did have real honey. It was an indie coffee shop in Portland. She didn't know for certain, however.

"Thank you for agreeing to meet with me," Tara said after a moment. "I appreciate it."

Lucius nodded at her, as if she was only giving him the courtesy due him.

As he didn't say anything more, Tara continued, "I figure this is something of an interview, to see if you are a good fit for my coven or not. I have questions for you, but I'm also certain that you have questions for me. Would you like to go first?"

Lucius gave her a small smile. "Thank you. Tell me about your battle with the Riprap man. The first time."

Tara blinked, surprised. That wasn't what she'd been expecting him to ask about. She picked up her cup and took a sip, regretting it instantly as the brew was just too bitter.

Lucius pointed a finger at her cup. Instantly, she saw a swirl of golden honey dance across the surface of the black tea. It moved on its own, dissolving into the hot liquid.

"Now try it," Lucius prompted.

Tara hesitated. Wasn't there a saying about not accepting honey from a stranger? She glanced up at him, only to see him staring at her closely.

Was this some sort of test? To see if she'd trust him or not?

While Tara didn't know or trust Lucius, Kyle did trust him. And Tara trusted Kyle.

She took a small sip of her tea. The honey had added the perfect level of sweetness, as well as the taste of some sort of fruit. "Orange blossom?" Tara asked after a second sip.

"Indeed," Lucius said. He seemed impressed despite himself.

"Thank you," Tara was sure to say as she put down her tea. Then she started talking about the Riprap man, how her soul had battled him deep under the water, on one of the footings of the Burnside bridge. He'd polluted the water, sliming her skin, stealing the light and her air.

Tara found it difficult to breathe as she relived the horror of that battle, the unnatural creature she faced, the blindness of the river "god"—Tara still maintained that it was a spirit, not a god. A true god wouldn't be so petty. Or so she hoped.

She explained her bargain, how she had promised to honor the spirit of the river at the equinox with rose petals. She'd set aside a large allotment, and had already planned on spending most of the day on a boat on the water, sprinkling the petals and singing hymns.

"After I got free, the river spirit appeared to attack the Riprap man. I'd assumed he hadn't survived, not until he showed up in my dreams last week." Tara grimaced and shuddered, remembering the coldness of the water.

"Water is your element, yes?" Lucius asked.

"It is," Tara said. "And I'm not going to let the Riprap man or anyone else keep me away from it." She'd consistently gone swimming ever since that battle, even though the first few times it had been difficult for her to put her head under the water, even at the shallow end of the pool at her local YMCA.

"Describe the Riprap man, his appearance, the last time you saw him," Lucius commanded.

Tara tried not to let his tone bother her. "It's as if the rocks that made up his body have been dislodged. He's no longer symmetrical. His torso is still stolid, but at the same time, I keep wondering if he's been weakened."

"The Riprap man's element is not water, correct?" Lucius said.

"I think that's right," Tara said, particularly given the reaction of the river spirit.

"Would you say that perhaps, given his appearance, his element might be earth? Or stone?"

Tara's eyes widened. "That hadn't occurred to me. But you're probably right." Why had the river spirit chosen someone like the Riprap man to be its champion when water wasn't the Riprap man's element?

"Given your description, it sounds to me that it's the water that's changed his appearance. As though the rocks have been in the path of a mighty torrent for decades, and are being slowly worn away," Lucius mused.

"That's an accurate description," Tara said, thinking about it. It made so much sense to her now.

"You may well be able to use that in your coming battle," Lucius said. "Calling the water to you. Though that may just provoke him into calling the stones that he's named himself after. An interesting dilemma."

"Will we still be battling? If I keep my promise to honor the spirit of the river?" Tara asked.

Lucius gave a cold laugh. "He'll prevent you from keeping your promise. You need to be prepared for that."

Tara nodded. She'd assumed that he'd try to stop her somehow. "I will still fight," she said.

"You are human. It's what you do best," Lucius said.

"Fighting against impossible odds. While any sane creature would accept that they've lost and move on."

"If you're so disdainful of humans, why would you want to join with us?" Tara said. "Why would you want to be considered for this coven?"

Lucius raised his eyebrows in surprise. "I'm not disdainful of your kind."

"Really?" Tara said, deliberately provoking him.

The sigh he gave her was worthy of any disgruntled teenager. "The majority of you aren't worth my time. Now, before you go off in a huff, let me explain."

He took a sip of his coffee while Tara tried to release her anger. Kyle had warned that Lucius could be difficult.

"My kind are long lived. Very long lived." He stared at her, his brilliant blue eyes taking on a pale light. She saw centuries in there. "How am I supposed to approach creatures who will only be around for a fraction of my lifetime? You're here, then gone. When I say you are not worthy of my time, I mean that literally. You rarely exist even long enough for me to notice you."

"I see," Tara said slowly.

"Do you? I doubt it," Lucius said dismissively.

"No, I do," Tara said. "When I was being tested, passing within the circles, the circle of earth, I had to become a tree. I had to experience the fall and winter, only to be reborn in the spring. An old oak led me through it."

"Interesting," Lucius said. "Kyle had said that I would find you fascinating. He may have been right. You're a strange mixture of natural and learned."

"Thanks, I think," Tara said. "Do you have more questions for me?"

Lucius cocked his head to the side as if the question itself puzzled him. "No, not at this time," he said slowly. "I assume you have questions for me?"

"I do," Tara said. She took a deep breath. She didn't want to piss Lucius off, but she had to make sure that he knew what he was getting into.

"The coven I'm forming is going to be different than a general witch's coven," she started with. "As you said, I'm a mixture of natural and learned, a hedgewitch who started off as a schooled witch. But one of the people I've invited is a pure hedgewitch."

Lucius raised a single imperial eyebrow at that but didn't say anything.

"I've also asked a mundane human to join us. He's a research librarian with mad skills. Since I have no ancient texts or lore, he's an incredibly useful resource for us, searching through old files and books. He has access to materials we don't."

"Fascinating," Lucius said. "Go on."

He actually did look interested. "Then there's Kaede. Ze is a fifth level witch who's left zir coven, who's an anarchist and runs a community center."

Lucius blinked. "I find it fascinating that humans have finally come to appreciate that gender is a continuum, not binary."

"Uhm, okay," Tara said, remembering that Kyle had emphasized more than once that Lucius wasn't really human. "What pronoun would you prefer? I apologize for not asking sooner."

That got her a real laugh, one that sounded warm and rich and full of honey. "He/his," Lucius said easily. "At least for today."

Tara wasn't sure if Lucius was being serious or not, if he really did change gender sometimes. "Thank you for telling me," she said. She took another sip of her tea. It was still perfect. "Then there's Kyle, who you know, and me."

"Are you the head of this coven?" Lucius asked.

"That's really the question of the hour, isn't it?" Tara said. "Generally, the head of a coven is the most powerful witch in the group. I'm not. I've only recently passed into the second level."

"I'm surprised by that," Lucius said. "I would have judged you as much stronger. You have the power." He paused, then asked, "Have you any familiars?"

"Kind of?" Tara said. She explained about Soot and how the Riprap man appeared to have captured the wind's attention.

"It makes sense that he'd have an affinity toward a familiar that was an element," Lucius said. "Given that he's already bound to a water spirit."

Tara sat up straighter. "Thank you," she said. "That explains a lot. But I don't know what to do. Do I try to call Soot back to me? Break the hold the Riprap man has on him? Or free the wind instead?"

"I can't advise you, I'm afraid," Lucius said. "I have had very few dealings with familiars and not a lot of insight. You might ask your other hedgewitch friend."

"I will ask her about it," Tara said, making a mental note.

"In the meanwhile, you might go about seeing if you can call a familiar for your current circle," Lucius said. "Some sort of fire element."

Tara opened her mouth and then shut it again. "What sort of creature takes the shape of a fire element?"

"That's something you'll have to discover, my dear," Lucius said. "I think that any sort of fire creature may help you in your coming battle."

Tara nodded, recalling the familiar spark deep in her core that still kept her warm. She'd developed an affinity for fire more recently, despite already having an affinity for water. What would it take to call a fire element? She was going to have to ask Kyle about it.

"So, for the sake of argument, say that I'm nominally in charge of this coven, though I'm going to listen to everyone and make this as much of a team effort as possible," Tara continued after a moment. "I think that strictly going by majority voting is a mistake." She knew that she'd end up fighting with Kaede on that point, but for now, Tara knew that she was right.

Tara turned a frank gaze on Lucius. "If I make a decision about something that you disagree with, will you follow my lead anyway? You probably have the strongest magic of the entire group."

"That depends," Lucius said. "If you've made an honest effort to listen to my council but still are convinced of your foolhardy ways, who am I to gainsay you? Though I will admit that if it happens frequently, I will be leaving your little group."

"Fair enough," Tara said. She swallowed. "Kyle has

said that you're a being of power, not human, quite alien and occasionally alarming. You've been very accommodating today, which I thank you for. But I need to understand exactly why Kyle finds you so disturbing."

"Ah, you want the mask to slip?" Lucius said. He considered for a long moment. "Very well."

He nodded, then grew very still.

Tara found herself swallowing against a suddenly dry throat. Lucius's physical appearance hadn't changed, though his eyes had taken on a brighter glow.

However, the *presence* that Lucius projected had completely transformed.

Tara gripped the edges of the table and held herself in place despite how fast her panic rose, her fight-or-flight instinct growing stronger by the second. It was as if she was suddenly face to face with a monster. Though Lucius hadn't said or done anything, and still looked human, Tara felt at a gut level that he was *alien* in a fundamental way, terrifying and dangerous, as if through will alone he could cause her harm.

He reminded her of the schizophrenic she'd seen at Hallowed Ground. He, too, had been frightening because he'd been so insane and high at the time, a danger to himself and others.

Lucius conveyed the same feeling to Tara, of imminent violence from the least provocation, just because someone said, "Hi" instead of "Hello."

And he wasn't human. Tara had no doubt about that, deep down in her bones.

They stared at each other across the table for an

endless time before Lucius put back on his mask, as it were, then reached down and took a sip of coffee.

Tara blinked and shook her head. With shaking hands she reached for her own mug. The tea warmed as she touched it, her hedgewitch magic suddenly at work.

She took a sip, then another, before she brought her eyes up to look at Lucius again.

"All better now?" he asked, his smile sardonic.

Tara nodded, not yet trusting her voice. After a few moments, she finally said, "Thank you for showing me."

She'd thought that the Riprap man had been an alien creature. She'd not really known what alien was, though, before Lucius had shown her.

"Any more questions?" Lucius said.

"No," Tara said. She pondered the being in front of her, who didn't appear to take offense at her sitting there thinking for a moment.

Could she work with Lucius? Invite him into her inner circle? Knowing that he was so alien, so magical, so malevolent at heart? Or would she feel as though she was using him, just to gain his power for her use?

"I can see your hesitation," Lucius said. "And I honor that, much more than if you had immediately leapt to invite me. My people are solitary in nature. I'm considered quite gregarious among my kind. Would it make a difference to you to know that I believe I would enjoy the company of your coven, at least for a while?"

"Yes," Tara said, taking a sigh of relief. "I hesitate because I don't want to feel as though I'm using you."

Lucius gave her a bitter smile. "And that's where our fundamental philosophies differ. I have no problem whatsoever using you for my gain. My automatic assumption is that you'll do the same. There would be no hard feelings about it. It's just in my nature."

"How would you be using us?" Tara asked, perplexed. He certainly didn't need their power or their magic.

"For entertainment, of course!" Lucius said snidely. "Plus, you do seem as though you might occasionally listen to the wisdom of your elders, which, believe me, is more rare than you can imagine."

"Would the Riprap man come after you? If he knew that you were a part of my coven?" Tara said after a bit. The part about being Lucius's entertainment stung. However, she'd rather know the truth.

The smile Lucius gave her reminded her of a cat having found its prey sitting unaware. "Oh, I'm counting on it."

Though Tara had originally invited everyone to Kyle's complex for the gathering on Monday night, Kaede had volunteered Hallowed Ground that evening for their meeting instead. The afterschool program finished at seven, and the people sleeping upstairs had been told that the downstairs was in use that night, something that happened now and again.

Kaede had left explicit instructions for Tara and the others to knock on the front door when they arrived.

Standing outside the converted office space, Tara still felt hesitant. It was as if the very building repelled her. She peered closely at the door, but couldn't see any markings on it. The night behind her felt soft, despite the soft pattering of rain. The smell of wet concrete filled the air. She shivered when a slight breeze touched the back of her neck, but when Tara turned around, she didn't see anyone, or anything, there.

Telling herself not to be ridiculous, Tara raised her hand and knocked, though her brain screamed at her that she was just inviting the monsters in by doing so.

Kaede opened the door immediately. "Felt you out there," ze said with a grin. "Wondered how long it would take for you to overcome the repulsion." Kaede wore skinny jeans and a plain gray sweatshirt, which made zir look younger.

"How did you do that?" Tara asked, curious. When Kaede closed the door, Tara saw the pentagram drawn in chalk on the inside, as well as sachets hanging inside each point of the star. "Ah," she said, nodding. That was what she'd felt.

The tables and chairs had all been pushed to the walls of the room, looking like the first time Tara had seen it. The air still held the remains of the meal that had been served, the potatoes and industrial gravy. Tara hoped that once she started working here, she could teach the ones who cooked how to spice the food better, make it less bland, more appetizing.

Kaede directed Tara to put her jacket on one of the chairs next to the door. The air was cooler than Tara had expected. The cold found her skin immediately, casting goosebumps across her shoulders, though she was dressed in a loose black sweater over a white shirt, jeans, and warm boots. Her soul liked this place: the room itself felt comfortable—homey, even. However, Tara still expected it to be warmer. Maybe that was because she associated comfort with warmth.

"Don't want the regulars coming by and knocking when they see lights on in the windows," Kaede explained about the door. "The charms should keep out the rest. Plus, it will let you know if anyone in the coven can't overcome the spells."

"I do have a mundane coming, Richard," Tara said, worried.

"Tell him to text you when he arrives," Kaede suggested.

Tara did that, only to receive a text a moment later with Richard saying, "I'm here."

Tara opened the door to find Richard standing there looking worried. "I know I've been here before but I just couldn't figure out if this was the right place or not." He stood rigidly still, his eyes wide in his pale face. He wore a black coat over his standard T-shirt and jeans.

He jumped when Tara reached out and wrapped her hand around his arm.

"It's the magic," Tara explained as she tugged him across the threshold.

"Wow," Richard said as he turned and took in the back of the door. "I mean, I know you have magic and all. I've experienced it. I just…Yeah."

Tara grinned at Kaede, who gave her a nod in return. "I'm Kaede," ze said. "This is my space."

"I can tell," Richard said as he shucked his coat,

putting it on one of the chairs next to the door, beside Tara's.

"Can you?" Tara asked. "Can you tell it's zir space? Or just that it's private?"

Richard thought for a moment. "Just private," he said after a moment.

Tara gave him an encouraging smile. She figured that would be his response. He was mundane, through and through.

Ginny arrived next. She had a big hug for Tara, which surprised her, though just a nod for the others. She wore a thick green wool jacket, with oversized sleeves and a long pointed hood—an elf jacket—over thick black leggings, solid boots, and a beige sweater that showed off her pale skin and copper hair.

After Tara introduced Ginny, she said, "I have a question for you, about my wind, Soot." Tara explained that what the Riprap man had done, how Tara hadn't been able to call Soot back since. The others listened intently.

"He's got ahold of it, that's fer sure," Ginny said, nodding. "Ye'll have to release him."

"How?" Tara asked, her heart sinking. She hadn't had Soot for long, but he still fit into her life, as if he'd filled a hole she hadn't known she had. She missed him more each day.

"Go to where ye called him. Open yer hands and spread yer arms and let 'im go," Ginny said. "Sorry, can't explain more than that. Just let 'im know your intent. That Riprap man will do the rest."

"Thanks," Tara said. One more thing to do before the equinox.

Lucius showed up next, wearing a timeless, scrumptious, long black wool coat over a black suit and white shirt. He had a cane with him that night, also black, with what appeared to be a silver dragon's head on the top of the cane.

"Interesting place," he said, looking sharply in all the corners, as if expecting large spiderwebs to be hanging there.

"Thank you," Kaede said through gritted teeth.

Tara had already warned all of them that Lucius sounded snide all the time. Each person in the coven needed to find their own relationship with him if this coven was going to work together.

Ginny, however, merely gazed at Lucius with wide eyes and had stammered hello when introduced.

Kyle came last. He'd insisted on going home after work, showering and changing before coming to the meeting. His mint-green long-sleeved shirt looked almost as formal as Lucius's suit, and set off Kyle's black skin nicely.

Had he felt the need to dress up for his sometimes lover? To show off? Tara wasn't certain.

Tara led them all to the center of the room. The floor had been washed clean, the pentagram no longer visible. The group stood in a circle. Though Tara knew she was supposed to be the main point, she felt as though Lucius drew all attention to himself, willfully or not. He stood directly opposite her, with Ginny and Kaede on either side of him. Richard and Kyle stood on either side of Tara.

Though Sheila and Miss Lucy had always stood in the center of the circle, drawing all the power to them, so they could focus it better, Tara deliberately stood with everyone else in the circle itself. That felt more right to her, and she suspected Kaede appreciated it as well.

"Thank you all for coming," Tara started off with. "I appreciate each and every one of you joining together in the circle tonight, to celebrate life and all its cycles. I call on the goddess Brigid to bless this endeavor, as she regularly blesses and guards the world with her grace and fortune. I call on the god Samil, warrior for all beings. I call on the fullness of the seasons, the turnings of the sun and the moon, the natural phases of the world everlasting, to witness our calling and our resolve," Tara said, her voice falling into a natural rhythm.

She hadn't planned out the prayer, though she knew she was supposed to. However, anytime she'd tried to do that, her words always came out stilted and monotone. She had some idea of what she wanted to say, then winged the rest of it, making sure to say "beings" instead of "people" where necessary.

Tara reached out to hold hands with Kyle, on her one side, and Richard, on her other. They in turn held hands with Kaede and Ginny, who reached out to Lucius last.

He made a face at her, but finally acquiesced, deigning to press his flesh against the mere humans.

A surge of warm power ran through the circle when

it was finally made whole. Tara had never felt such a strong connection before.

Was this due to Lucius? Or was it because she'd chosen all these beings to be part of *her* coven? In the past, would she have felt something this strong if the leader of the coven had joined in the circle, instead of standing in the center of it?

Tara called on the moon to bless them, then directed the flow of power outward to heal the world. It was surely needed it at this point, though Tara realized that even their combined magical healing was just a drop in the bucket being rapidly emptied by man.

In a regular circle, the head witch would focus the magic thrumming through her and direct it toward some task. She hadn't really been able to think of anything that she wanted to get done, except to stop the Riprap man.

Would the magic being generated stop her enemy? Could they, as a group, utterly destroy him? She wasn't sure. She knew, though, that once she wielded that knife, destroyed another being with power, she'd never let it go.

Though Tara had left Miss Lucy, the allure of dark forces still haunted her.

Instead, Tara nodded to Kaede, who spoke, starting a new prayer. Effortlessly, ze picked up the threads of magic flowing between them and wove them together into a broad net. Tara couldn't see it with her physical eyes, but she had a sense of it, golden and glittering, expanding as it floated above the circle.

Then Kaede flung the net up, pushing the healing

and goodwill through the ceiling, up toward those sleeping above them.

Tara admired zir skill, how ze shaped the power with words and prayers, bringing not just blessing but actual healing for those who were physically inside the structure Kaede commanded.

When Kaede finished, Tara said a closing prayer, thanking everyone again, before releasing the hands of those standing beside her.

"Wow," was all Ginny had to say, looking around the circle at everyone. "Is it always like that?" she asked. She sounded stoned. Tara felt the same way.

"No, not always," Tara said. "This is a particularly strong group."

"Pity," Lucius said. "I would consider joining more covens after you've passed if it was," he explained after a moment.

That made Tara smile. It seemed that even Lucius had been impressed by what they'd just done.

Kaede nodded. "It's because of the loose structure of the group," ze said, nodding zir head. "The tight hierarchy of the regular circle usually chokes off the flow of power."

Tara wasn't about to roll her eyes but honestly, she didn't think that was the case at all. She strongly believed that it was because of their combined power, due to a large part because of Lucius.

Richard looked lost. "Can someone explain to the blind guy what just happened?"

Lucius looked him up and down. "Despite being blind, as you so aptly described it, you actually contributed a small trickle of power to the rest of us. We, in turn, cast a healing for the poor souls who inhabit in this building. I believe that come morning, they may find that their reliance on drugs and other crutches has been greatly diminished. Well done," he added, nodding toward Kaede.

Though his words sounded like an insult, Kaede accepted them with grace.

"I've never been part o'something so strong," Ginny commented. "Not even dancing on the solstice with me gran during the full moon."

"Did we actually heal people?" Richard asked, still trying to figure out what he'd been a part of.

"Yes," Tara said. "We couldn't—we couldn't completely heal them. That would have taken too much energy—more than even this group could manage. But we did help all of those sleeping above us."

"Wow," Richard said. "I feel as though I've just run three marathons. But also as if I raised a million bucks by finishing. You know?"

Tara grinned at him. "I know." She turned to Lucius. "Were you able to feel each thread of power individually?"

"Yes," Lucius said. "Vaguely," he added with a dismissive gesture.

Tara found that interesting. She hadn't been able to figure out which strand of power came from which being—it had all flowed together like a grand river.

"If that's all the fun and games for tonight, then?" Lucius asked Tara.

"Yes, yes it is. Thank you for coming," she added.

"We'll be back together Wednesday night." The night of the equinox. The night when the Riprap man would be coming for her soul.

For the first time in more than a week, Tara felt hope.

CHAPTER 7

The river god had warned me about the transformation, telling me that it would induce a great deal of pain. I don't believe He understands the mortal agony of blood boiling away under the skin or bones crushing together into a new form. My shrieks and screams must have sounded as though I was being tortured by the devil himself. I cannot say how long the transformation took: a single night, or an entire eternity. Perhaps both. My new form is not displeasing to me, the rocks and boulders reminding me of the headwaters before me. However, Mulinohana appears dissatisfied with my new appearance. Perhaps He expected something different? I shall endure, though, as long as my new form shall last. Not forever, no, even mountains will be ground down to dust eventually. But I have promised to serve my new God until that day.

Wilson Evermore, Reborn and Everlasting, 1921

AS SOON AS Kyle and Tara returned to Kyle's condo after the magical healing circle at Hallowed Ground, Tara stepped out onto the porch to release Soot. She felt both wired and exhausted. However, she also felt as if she had to let go of the wind as soon as she could. She'd never had asthma, but she imagined that it probably felt like this, unable to take a deep breath at least half the time.

Tara placed her own protection sachet on the porch railing, filled with angelica and Scottish thistle, hiding her from prying eyes. She called Soot, not expecting him to show up.

A wind swirled around her jacket and the dog appeared at her feet.

"Good boy," Tara said. Should she let him go? Now that he'd finally come to her call? Just seeing him filled her heart with a warm joy.

Soot pushed up against her hand, wanting to be petted. Her fingers followed the cool contours of his head, her fingers sliding across his soft fur. His tail thumped on the hard concrete of the balcony.

"Soot, you know I can't keep you," she said softly.

He merely looked up at her, as if awaiting her command. Did she want him to go chase something? Anything?

Tara took a step back. "I release you," she said. She opened her hands, palms out. Then she pushed her arms skyward, as if doing a yoga pose. "I release you," she said again. "You are no longer at my beck and call. Off with you. Be free."

Her arms raised above her head, Tara said again, "I release you."

She brought her hands down in front of her, palms together in prayer pose, closing her eyes. "I release you," she whispered again.

Winds whirled around and around, pressing against her legs, tugging at her ponytail, begging to be noticed.

"I release you," Tara said firmly, stubbornly.

Finally, the winds died down. Tara opened her eyes to find herself standing alone on the balcony.

Had it worked? She took a deep breath, her chest still slightly constricted, though not as much.

She regretted having to let Soot go. He remained special to her. She wished she could call him again. She pressed her lips together so that she wouldn't.

Damn it. She didn't like this part at all.

Maybe after she defeated the Riprap man she could call Soot back to her. She hoped so.

Blinking back tears that she didn't want to feel, Tara went back into the warm living room, ignoring the way the winds appeared to push at the windows for the rest of the night.

Tara breathed a sigh of relief when she let herself into Ye Olde Magicke Shoppe and saw that there was a large stuffed manila envelope with her name on it waiting for her at the counter. She quickly put her lunch into the refrigerator in the backroom of the shop, got the money for the register out of the safe in the supply room, counted it out, signed for it, as well as opened the shop for customers before she ripped open the end of her package.

The heady scent of roses flowed up and out of the container. Tara peered down at them.

Wait, was that something moving?

She shook the bag, then nearly dropped it when black beetle-like bugs came to the top of the pink and red petals.

They were eating her petals! Where had they come from? How had they gotten in there?

Tara was about to take the package into the backroom and blast the petals with a cleaning spell— maybe some lemon balm, rosemary, and angelica would do the trick—when the bell announcing customers merrily rang.

For the next three hours, Tara dealt with a steady stream of people coming into the shop. It was too early for Halloween; however, that appeared to be what everyone was shopping for. Wands and witch's hats and trinkets for decorating their houses.

By the time Tara got back to her packet of rose petals again, it was a heaving mass of beetles. The package wiggled in between her fingers.

Ugh! She couldn't clean the bugs out. The petals were ruined. She was just going to have to throw them all away.

Luckily, she had another stash of petals at home. They were under protective spells, or at least had been since she realized the Riprap man was still alive and coming after her.

The first thing she was going to have to do when she got home was to check that those petals were still okay.

Then the shop went crazy again, another stream of customers arriving.

When Tara had a few moments to breathe midafternoon, she went into the backroom of the shop to check on the jar of rose petals there.

While the front room catered to simple tourists with its pyramids of power, charged crystals and geodes, as well as focusing wands and protective rocks, the backroom held ingredients that real witches and beings of power used. The backroom was hidden in plain sight according Patricia, the owner of the shop—the only people who went back there, or who even noticed that it existed, were people who had magic in them.

Tara relaxed as soon as she stepped into the clean space. Brown wooden shelves lined the walls and held cannisters of ingredients. An old-fashioned balance stood on the counter in the corner, with the metal weights beneath it. Two large, silver refrigerators lurked in the corner, holding the fresh herbs.

With trepidation, Tara opened the fridge and picked up the cannister that contained the rose petals. She shook it, but didn't hear any scrabbling.

Cautiously, Tara opened the container. It still smelled like roses. She shook it gently.

No bugs spoiled the pink and red petals.

Tara measured out four cups of rose petals into a clean bag. Luckily they didn't cost that much, only a few dollars per cup; however, Tara didn't want to clean out all of Patricia's supply either. She carefully sealed the bag, labeled it with her name, then taped a sprig of rosemary to the outside, to help preserve the petals inside.

Of course, when Patricia arrived (late) Tara was in such a hurry to gather up her things that she forgot the package in the backroom. She didn't discover this until after she'd gotten back to Kyle's condo, after the store was closed and she was checking on her own supply.

"Can you believe that I forgot them?" Tara told Kyle, grousing about her day.

He raised both eyebrows at her. "It might not have just been coincidence. Would you call what happened to you bad luck?"

Tara nodded. Then understanding dawned on her. "It's the Riprap man, isn't it? A spell of bad luck has been cast on me."

"Exactly," Kyle said. "He's going to do everything he can to prevent you from honoring your promise to the river spirit."

Tara looked at her pitifully small collection of rose petals. She'd expected to have a dozen cups or more. Now, she had merely four. She was going to have to make every petal count.

Or else face the Riprap man in battle for her soul, once again.

TARA ANXIOUSLY CHECKED HER ROSE PETALS IN THE morning, but no beetles appeared to have found them. Then again, she had put extra protection spells on and around the container. Kyle had contributed a couple of sachets as well.

Fortunately, Tara kept the container holding the petals—a solid white cannister originally designed to hold coffee—closed as she made her way from her room to the kitchen. An unseen line in the floor tripped her, sending her sprawling on her face, flinging the cannister in front of her.

Fearing the worst, Tara ignored her bruised elbows and knees and crawled over to check the container. Luckily, it hadn't shattered on impact. A large crack did now run across the base of it. She was able to transfer the petals, still bug free, from the porcelain container to a glass jar. Then she thought better of it, and put them into one of Kyle's plastic disposable containers instead.

When Tara tripped and fell again not two minutes later, she was glad of her choice. Normally, she wouldn't keep any herbs or ingredients in plastic. It was too porous, let in too much light and air, which would degrade the ingredients kept inside. But for a single day, Tara was glad to use it.

Now, she just had to get to the boat pier on time, without dropping or losing her petals. Her protection sachet for the day mostly held goldenseal as a charm against bad luck, as well as hellebore, ginseng, and rue to guard her from evil. However, they didn't seem to be doing much to counter whatever it was the Riprap man was doing.

Tara dressed in a lightweight gray sweater, along with a bright blue rain jacket that would keep off any wind or water. She wore her rainbow patterned rainboots, along with her sunhat. The day outside was clear again, but Tara didn't trust the clouds on the horizon, promising plenty of rain later on. Crisp air reddened her cheeks and lifted her ponytail up from her back.

Tara had paid for a tourist type boat trip that day, traveling up and down the river so she could scatter her petals properly. Though the trip to the pier where she'd meet the boat should have only taken an hour, she left two hours early due to her bad luck.

Of course, the MAX train she boarded ground to a halt between stations. She ended up sitting for almost thirty minutes before it got moving again. Which made her miss her bus connection.

Tara clutched her bag to her like she was a crazed woman, never putting it beside her once. She knew that the moment she released it, she might forget it or someone would steal her petals.

The walk to pier was more empty than she'd expected. Not even the homeless were on the sides of the road. It felt eerie to walk along such an empty street, even half a block. Small one-story buildings were on either side, the front windows dark and sightless. Winds carrying the smell of rotting fish and reeds swirled around her. Clouds covered the sun, turning the day abruptly gray and chilled.

Tara kept looking over her shoulder, expecting to see the Riprap man or Soot or hell, even Lucius stalking behind her.

The street remained empty. Tara wondered it if was just her imagination or if it was part of the general spell the Riprap man had put on her that made her want to turn tail and run.

With great relief, Tara finally reached the small building from which she'd bought her ride. She'd called the night before to make sure that everything was still on track. The harried woman who'd answered had assured Tara that it was all still a go.

The gray siding on the walls had seen better days. Dirt-spattered raindrops covered the front windows. However, a faded red sign proclaiming the place as "Open" had been turned in the window for the door.

Tara opened the door with trepidation. "Hello?" she called into the empty office.

Two desks sat behind the tall counters. Piles of paper filled the desks and not in an orderly chaos. Ancient yellowing monitors sat on each desk. Cheap wood paneling covered the walls, and the air smelled like tacky pine air-fresheners.

"Hello?" Tara called again. She knew she was early for her appointment, but only by fifteen minutes.

She looked behind her, but there were no chairs for her to sit on. Just calendars at least five years out of date on the wall, showing washed-out pictures of boats gliding across the water on formerly sunny days.

From somewhere in the back of the building, Tara heard the sound of water gushing through plumbing. Finally, an older woman stuck her head out into the front office—April, if Tara was remembering correctly.

"Ah, Tara, you're finally here," April said. She had gray hair that stood at attention all around her face, with watery gray eyes set deeply into a tanned face. Her lipstick was an unfortunate pale pink, something that would have looked better on a teenager, not someone approaching sixty.

"Jacob has the boat all set and ready to go," April continued. She started sorting through the papers on the desk on the left side of the office, first looking at the papers at the top of one pile before shifting to the next. "Now, where did that final release form go?"

Tara kept a tight smile on her face. More bad luck? It appeared so. April had to reprint the forms for Tara to sign after fifteen minutes of fruitless search.

"Don't tell Jacob," April asked as Tara finally finished signing all the forms. "He'll scold me for them getting lost. I really did print them out once before," she assured her.

Tara didn't bother explaining that it was a supernatural creature affecting all of them. "I'm sure they'll show up as soon as I step out of the office," she said.

April gave a bright laugh. "Isn't that how it always goes! Now, here's your copy. Hurry down the pier. You'll see The Yellow Rose midway down, in berth 39, on the left."

"Thank you," Tara said. She didn't think that Jacob would leave without her. She'd expected to be one of the few paying customers that day. It was late in the season, and there wouldn't be that many tourists who wanted to go out on the river these days.

However, that turned out to be wrong. A group of twelve schoolchildren, around the age of ten, were already on the boat, along with half a dozen harried looking adults.

"Good, you got here," Jacob said, taking Tara's paper from her with one hand while helping her over the bow on the other. "I wouldn't have left without you, as it was our fault that the time was changed and you weren't notified."

"I see," Tara said. The kids all looked sulkily at her, predisposed to dislike her for having made them wait.

This was going to be even more awkward than she'd imagined. If she could have turned around and walked right back off the boat, she would have.

How was she going to sing praises to the river spirit while a bunch of kids watched? How could she keep them from disturbing her?

Tara cursed the Riprap man once again while making her way to a side bench. She was just going to have to figure out a way to make this work regardless.

TARA'S FIRST BREAK CAME WHEN THE TEACHERS AND volunteers gathered all the kids to the front of the boat for their midmorning snack of cheese sticks and juice. Tara wasn't about to point out that hyping the kids up on the sugary drink probably wasn't the smartest move. However, at least it gave her a few minutes at the back of the boat alone.

Tara gave a sigh of relief when she opened the plastic container with the rose petals. They were still pure, no sign of bugs or beetles.

She grabbed a handful out of the container, then closed it up again immediately. For a moment, Tara closed her eyes and composed herself. Then she opened her eyes, looking out on the peaceful water flowing behind the boat and started quietly singing a hymn to the water spirits, thanking them for the mighty water for bringing all things life.

As she reached the end of short hymn, Tara reached out over the edge of the boat and opened her palm, intending to drop the first fistful of rose petals onto the surface of the water.

A sudden wind sprang up. The petals streamed to the nearest bank in a solid line instead of floating down to the water.

"Damn it!" Tara said. She guiltily looked behind her. Hopefully none of the kids, or their minders, had heard her.

She grabbed a few more petals, merely stating, "Thank you for your bounty," before she tried scattering them again.

This time, she actually saw Soot flowing through the air, snatching up every petal and sending it onward.

"Oh, Soot," Tara said. Her heart beat harder and a familiar ache set in. She abruptly realized that she hadn't let him go, not completely. However, he wasn't really hers to direct either.

The dog looked at her happily, as if they were playing the best game in the world. Anytime she let go of even a few petals, he chased them all away from the water. Then he would come back and sit at her feet, looking proud of his accomplishment and begging for more of this game.

Tara gave up after a while. She had barely a handful of petals left. Maybe she should just jump in the water with them in her hand?

When Tara peered down into the water, the face of the Riprap man grinned back up at her.

If she went into the water, he'd drag her down into the depths. Maybe she'd survive a physical battle with him. Chances were, she wouldn't.

What was she going to do? How was she going to scatter her rose petals across the water? It might have just been her imagination, but she felt as though the river spirit was growing tired of her failure.

Then the kids broke free from their imposed gathering, having finished their snack, and came racing back to the rear end of the boat again.

Tara leaned against the railing, her own dark cloud descending. There had to be a way for her to get at least a few petals into the water, without Soot chasing them all away, without the Riprap man dragging her into the depths like a waiting crocodile.

But how?

WHEN THE BOAT HAD FINALLY FINISHED ITS TOUR, TARA still had no idea what she was going to do. There were bridges, of course, that she could use for flinging her petals into the water, but Soot would be sure to stop her. What would happen if she went to the very edge of the riverbank and just stuck her hand into the water? She knew that she'd promised to scatter the rose petals across the surface of the river. Hopefully if she managed to scatter at least a few petals, that would satisfy Mulinohana.

Tara wasn't about to admit failure. Not yet. Though she knew that if she didn't appease the river spirit, it wouldn't help her when the Riprap man came to battle for her soul.

She suspected that it was just revenge driving the Riprap man. He wouldn't bind Tara to one of the bridges, but instead, would kill her just to prove a point, to prove that he was a better disciple of Mulinohana than she was, despite her affinity for water.

Most of the riverbank in the city itself had been built up, not just to prevent flooding but also to prevent accidental drowning. The city didn't want to be sued every time an irresponsible parent let their kid near the water. So the city officials had made access to the water difficult.

Tara ended up taking a cab to one of the boat launching areas south of the city. It looked like a driveway leading down to the water. Trees rustled on either side of Tara as she marched down the concrete. Cold winds blew off the river, making her shiver. The sound of constant traffic flowed behind her, people rushing home after a long day at the office.

Of course, Tara tripped before she got to the end of the launch point. The container of rose petals flew open as she flung it up into the air, the petals streaming out to either side, scattered among the tall weeds growing beside the driveway.

"Goddess take you!" Tara cursed as she carefully picked at her bleeding palms, trying to remove some of the small pieces of gravel imbedded there. Her jeans had torn on impact as well, and her knees were bloody.

Groaning, Tara forced herself back up, picking up the plastic container that sat at the water's edge. Almost all of the petals were gone. She was able to scratch half a dozen petals that had stuck to the inside of the container out with her fingernails.

Instead of being fresh and fragrant, the few petals that remained were creased and torn. Hardly an adequate offering.

Still, Tara did her best. She sat at the edge of the water and sang the praises of the water and the river spirit, thanking him yet again for his bounty as well as his restraint, for not flooding the city, for granting them passage along the waters. Finally, Tara grit her teeth and stuck her hand into the water, releasing the few petals she had managed to save.

She saw them float back up, onto the surface of the river, then swirl away against the current.

It wasn't enough.

The battle was coming.

And she'd just blown her best chance of weakening the Riprap man.

~

"I FAILED," TARA ANNOUNCED GLUMLY WHEN SHE MET with the coven later that evening. They'd gathered at a coffee shop just up the road from Hallowed Ground. Tara wrapped her carefully salved and bandaged hands around her tea cup and explained what had happened to the group.

"Does he come for ye tonight? Or in the morning?" Ginny asked when Tara finished. The light sprinkling of rain they'd walked through still sparkled in her bright red hair.

"Last time, it was the evening after the solstice," Tara said. "So I think I'm safe tonight. I don't think he wants to use my soul, like he has the other witches. Instead, this is just revenge, because the water spirit chose me instead of him."

"Do you think it's possible that the Riprap man injured Mulinohana during their battle?" Lucius asked. He sat slightly apart from the rest of the group, his chair pushed back with a general air of disdain.

Tara blamed herself for his reaction. He might not have been so put out if she'd actually managed to honor the river spirit as she'd promised. Then again, he'd known that the Riprap man would try to stop her.

Ginny answered. "He might have. If this Mulinohana is just a spirit in search of a human to bond with."

"How did they bond in the first place? Why?" Richard asked. He was rapidly taking notes on his phone, research angles he wanted to explore.

"Perhaps he was the only one in the area at the

time," Lucius said. "As I understand it, bonding is very place specific, correct?"

"Aye," Ginny said. "And if this Riprap man was at the headwaters when Mulinohana lost its other followers, it might have just chosen from the lot at hand."

"And the Riprap man is strong, right?" Kaede said. "Wouldn't the spirit have chosen the strongest available to it?" Ze presented zir question with the air of a student discussing an upcoming paper.

"Maybe. Maybe not," Kyle said. He shrugged when Tara threw a questioning glance his way. "I've been asking around, making inquiries about hedgewitches and their familiars."

Tara smiled at that. The Riprap man just happened to have a familiar that was stronger than most, the spirit of the Willamette River.

"I tried releasing Soot, the wind who I'd bound," Tara said to the group. "I really didn't release him, though. I'm not sure why, if it was because I didn't really want to let go, or because I was doing it wrong, or something else." She took a deep breath, then turned to Ginny. "Is it possible to break the bond between a witch and their familiar?"

Ginny looked at her with big eyes. "It's possible. Anything's possible. It just ain't easy."

Lucius raised his hand to draw the attention of the group, but then just sat there with his lips pressed together, not saying anything.

After a few moments of silence, he finally gave Tara

a vicious smile. "How do you feel about being a distraction, my dear?" he asked.

Tara blinked. She hadn't expected that question at all. "As long as I don't end up being dead or forever soulless, I'm game."

"I can't guarantee your safety," Lucius said seriously. "We can only give you a fighting chance."

"I'll take it," Tara said.

Even a slight hope was better than none.

CHAPTER 8

Though my new form delights me still, I have learned of a few drawbacks. I had never been intimate with a woman before, never having felt a grand desire, as well as wanting to save myself for matrimony. Now, I shall never know the delights of the flesh. I cannot hold onto the illusion of a man during intimacy. Even if I found a woman willing to bear my true foreboding nature, I no longer function as a regular man. It is yet another sacrifice I gladly make to the great river god Mulinohana. I wish only to please my chosen god, to protect the grand city of Portland, and to continue to marvel at the progress marching across the land daily. I do not let myself dwell on my faults, how difficult it is to commune with Mulinohana sometimes, how the witches fight me when they should be begging me to take their spoiling souls and dedicate their lives toward true goodness. But I shall prevail.

Wilson Evermore, Transformed Protector, 1936

TARA SPENT the morning preparing for her possible death. She already had a will, courtesy of the first time she'd fought the Riprap man. She called her mom, just to chat. Her parents had "retired" and now owned a hobby farm in Wisconsin. It was always fascinating to hear about their latest project. Tara had never considered her parents "handy" but they'd fully committed to the farm.

That morning, Tara had made herself a bright tea, starting with a base of organic green tea, then adding dried lemongrass, dried blueberries, and dried apple bits. She smoothed it out with a touch of vanilla and cinnamon. Though the morning was sunny, it wasn't warm. Tara had brought a thick blanket with her to wrap around herself as she sat out on the balcony sipping her tea and staring at the buildings in front of her.

She felt as though she'd had too many last days. She wasn't frantic this time. Instead, she felt resigned to her fate. She wasn't planning on dying, but she also wasn't fighting so hard for every minute, either.

Tara made the decision to start planning for her future. She made appointments to go see new apartments for both that day as well as later in the week. She wrote a long, impassioned email to Miss Lucy to ask for donations of ingredients to Hallowed Ground, so Tara could start helping the youth there.

Then, determinedly, Tara took herself to the Y for a good long swim. The smell of the chlorine as she walked into the building made her shoulders drop down as she relaxed. The waters of the pool itself looked blue and inviting. A water aerobics class for seniors was being taught along the front side of the pool, while the back was separated off into lanes for people to swim laps.

Tara felt her world suddenly right itself as she slipped into the water. *This* was right. *This* was home. When Tara had been much younger, she'd wondered if her spirit animal would be an otter or a porpoise, some type of water creature. However, she now realized that *she* was the water creature, herself. After she finished her laps, she spent some time on the other side of the lap lanes, treading water and just splashing around, playing, all the while ignoring the women glaring at her from the class.

When Tara finally left the water, she felt refreshed despite all the exercise she'd just had. She was still humming as she took a shower and washed her hair, cleaning off the chlorine. She'd take another shower later, as the evening approached, to clean and purify herself for the coming ordeal.

She knew she shouldn't feel as buoyant as she did. This was possibly her last day on earth. But she couldn't help herself.

Tara slowed as she passed the long information desk just inside the door. A "help wanted" sign hung on the front of the desk, something she hadn't noticed on her way in.

It seemed that her local Y was looking for a fulltime swim instructor.

Tara stopped and asked Casey—the tall African

American woman who generally worked mornings. She was enthusiastic about Tara getting the position, insisting that she fill out an application right then.

"But my certifications for First Aid aren't current," Tara felt obliged to point out.

Casey pointed to the part of the job description that said that the Y would "facilitate the process of getting certified." Then she continued, saying, "You're the right person. You'd live in that pool if you could."

Tara grinned and nodded, acknowledging that Casey was right. "I'll apply," Tara said. She'd taught swimming lessons to kids before, as well as adults. She was certain that she could work around the hours that she needed to give to Hallowed Ground. And it would be the perfect match for her.

The job didn't pay well, but Tara had never needed a lot to live on. She'd be able to get by.

Excited by the prospect, Tara walked back out into the sunny day. She had too much going right at this point for her to lose the upcoming battle.

TARA SAT ON THE LEATHER COUCH IN THE EMPTY CONDO watching the black night through the sliding glass doors leading out to the balcony. She still smelled the lovely chicken curry she'd prepared for herself. It wasn't her ideal last meal—that would have been a ribeye, medium rare, with broccoli drenched in butter and garlic, along with a huge salad and a good glass of red wine.

The chicken curry was a good placeholder, however.

It left her with yet one more thing to look forward to after the battle.

She found she missed Kyle more than she'd expected. He'd stood by her through the first battle, taking care of her physical body while her soul battled with the Riprap man.

However, he'd gathered with the others at Hallowed Ground, forming a powerful circle to aid her. She just had to keep the Riprap man distracted while they did their thing.

Tara pulled her ratty bathrobe more closely around her. She'd finished her peppermint tea and now sat quietly, humming snatches of hymns as they came to her.

Her phone sat beside her on the couch. She already had a text written out. She just needed to send it.

It felt to Tara as if a door or a window had just opened, letting a cold breeze blow through the warm condo. She glanced over her shoulder, wondering if Kyle had forgotten something, but the door leading to the hallway was still closed.

When she turned back around, the Riprap man stood on the balcony, outside the sliding glass doors. He wore his true shape, with boulders piled one on top of the other to form the rough form of his torso, arms, and legs. He still looked lopsided, as if the stones had been forced out of place. His ancient bowler sat jauntily on the back of his bare skull, as if he were some sort of gentleman caller.

Tara sent her text quickly.

The Riprap man was making a beckoning motion with his hand when she looked up.

Tara felt herself rise, cool air kissing her bare skin and raising goosebumps all across her shoulders and chest. She looked down, not surprised to discover that she was nude.

The circle around her belly where the fire had burned her during her last battle suddenly warmed and swelled up. She often forgot it was there, as it had faded back into her flesh.

When she glanced back, she saw her body slumped on the couch, her eyes closed, her mouth slightly open. It looked as though she was sleeping. Hopefully she wouldn't drool too much.

Tara floated through the glass of the closed door. The temperature didn't change, though she knew it was much colder outside than it had been inside.

"I have come to take your soul," the Riprap man told her in a clear voice.

"You'll have to fight me for it," Tara assured him. She sounded more confident than she felt, facing the creature before her. "And you'll lose. Like you did the last time."

"Ah, but the last time, you were aided by the great Mulinohana. This time, you must battle me alone," the Riprap man said with smug satisfaction. "I will prove to the river god that his choice of champion was ill suited to the task. As you have already proven."

Tara shrugged. "I'm sorry about that," she said softly. "I did try."

"You failed," the Riprap man said, glee tinging his

voice. "And now you will pay for your interfering ways."

Though Tara wanted to point out that she wasn't the one who'd interfered the day before when she'd been trying to sprinkle her rose petals over the waters, she didn't.

Instead, she gave what she hoped was an evil smile to the Riprap man. She'd been practicing all afternoon, trying to channel some of Lucius's animosity. From the way the Riprap man suddenly blinked, she knew she'd succeeded.

"Bring it," she challenged.

Darkness came rushing at her and Tara felt herself falling into an endless black hole.

Tara found herself standing beside a wildly rushing river, the sound of it deafening. Huge boulders stuck up out of the water, the tops covered in slimy moss. The sky had turned gray and overcast, iron cold and misting. Dark, ominous woods stretched out on either side of the river, with brambles cutting off any paths that might be found between the trees. Cold mud squished up between her toes.

Though Tara had never been here, she knew the place instantly: These were the very headwaters of the Willamette river.

The Riprap man came roaring up from behind her, intent on grabbing her and tossing her into the water.

Though it was just her soul here, she knew that she'd never survive being battered in those rapids.

Tara dropped down into a crouch. The Riprap man missed his grip, slipping himself on the wet mud, sending them both crashing to the ground. He kept trying to grapple her, while she tried to squirm away.

Why was he using a physical attack? It didn't make any sense to Tara. Why wasn't he attacking her magically? Streaks of cold mud covered her skin, chilling her to her faraway bones.

Then she tried to pull up the fire she felt was always banked inside her. All she managed was a small spark, a flare that warmed her abruptly then faded away.

The Riprap man still let go of her, flinching back as if he'd been burned. "Your tricks will not work," he assured her. "Mulinohana reigns here."

"Why bring me to the headwaters?" Tara asked as she drew herself to her feet. She stayed crouched down in a squat, ready to drop to her knees if the Riprap man rushed her.

"So that Mulinohana can watch your defeat," the Riprap man said.

"No, it's so that you can rededicate yourself to your god," Tara said. "He's turned his back on you, making you wait until the equinox. But he still won't allow you to rebind yourself to him. Not unless you can actually kill me."

Beady black eyes narrowed at Tara. "You are too smart for a woman," he commented.

Tara snorted. "Get with the times. We have the right to vote and everything."

"Not for long," the Riprap man promised. "Or at least, you won't." He ran at her again.

Tara was prepared this time. Instead of staying crouched and grappling with him again, she leaped up, flying high, landing on the nearest boulder.

The moss beneath her bare feet was warmer than she would have expected. It also was less slimy. She balanced on the rock without effort.

The Riprap man paused on the bank instead of leaping up after her. He halted at the side of the riverbank, looking askance at the rapidly rushing water.

Tara was surprised that he didn't just jump up after her. What was he playing at? Were the rocks too far away from the earth for him to feel comfortable? She realized that she'd always seen him with his feet on the ground. He'd always marched around her and never swam.

"Afraid of the water?" Tara taunted from where she stood, out of reach. "But I thought the water god was your best buddy."

Growling, the Riprap man crouched down, gauging the distance from the river bank to where she stood.

Tara crouched herself. She knew she couldn't pass him in midair, switching places with him. That kind of thing only happened in chop-socky movies. She still timed her leap to match his, jumping to the side and landing squarely on the next boulder.

The Riprap man grabbed for her, but missed. He didn't even come close. He wavered back and forth, trying to get his feet under him.

"Balance," Tara taunted. "That's what water is all

about. The balance between things." She remembered her fight with the water when she was walking the circles. She couldn't overwhelm such a mighty force. She'd passed within the fire, giving herself to it. The water would have washed her away. Instead, she'd needed to find the fine line between compliance and force.

"You don't have any balance in your life," Tara told the Riprap man. "You only know force. That is the way of rocks, stubbornly sitting in the way or plummeting down on top of you. The river is subtle. Water always finds a way through."

She knew that she wasn't speaking merely for him, but also for the benefit of the river spirit. They were at the headwaters. She still had a chance to prove that she was the more worthy companion.

"You are a fool," the Riprap man said. "You know nothing of power. The mighty Willamette destroyed the city of Portland many times before I came, before my sacrifices."

"What sacrifices?" Tara asked. "Because from here, all it looks like is that you killed a bunch of innocent witches. You forced your way through there, instead of making better bargains."

"I gave my life to the river." The Riprap man spoke vehemently. "I gave it everything. My body. My soul. To protect that great city."

"Your sacrifices were useless," Tara scorned. "Man straightened out the river. Built the dams. It was only through his works that the floods stopped. Not because of some bargain you made," Tara said. She'd done the research. The problem had been addressed far upriver of the city.

"No, you are wrong," the Riprap man said. He swayed where he stood, as if the water still buffeted him, though he was standing far above it. "My sacrifices were worth it."

While the Riprap man spoke, Tara turned her attention back toward the riverbank. Could she jump back from where she stood? Maybe. She asked Hayvu—the goddess of the western wind—to carry her away on strong winds as she leaped again.

The bank seemed to slide further away as Tara flew through the air. She felt herself clawing through the air, willing herself to solid earth.

The sound of the Riprap man behind her made her focus her will harder, sharpening the point of her awareness to a knife's point.

To her surprise, a smaller, more solid wind pushed her the last few inches so she landed on solid ground.

Tara didn't see Soot when she looked around. She still felt as though the wind had helped, and was able to take deeper breaths because he'd been there.

Now, standing on the cold mud, Tara faced the Riprap man. She would have thought that he'd be more comfortable standing on the rocks that resembled him. He looked worried, though.

"You will stop chasing me," Tara told him as she pushed her awareness under the cold waters rushing in front of her.

"Or else what?" the Riprap man sneered.

The voice of the water was so loud! It was difficult

to hear him. When Tara tore her awareness away, she saw that he'd crouched down and was about to jump over to where she stood.

"I don't want to kill you," Tara said plainly.

"I'm sure you will be eulogized for your restraint at your wake," the Riprap man taunted.

"Destroying you, dislodging one rock from the other, breaking the bindings that hold you in a single form, isn't that difficult," Tara pointed out. While she didn't necessarily have the power herself, she knew that when she stood with the rest of her coven, she might.

She imagined the process, how a strong current would strike the Riprap man just under his chest, where his ribs would be, where the rock was already unbalanced. A wash of magic with a blow of pure power would start his torso crumbling. More jets of water would take apart his wrists and elbows. Bits of his body would fall, crushing his feet and ankles. His head would fall last, shattering as it struck the ground, the bowler hat rolling off to the side, undamaged.

Though the rock was too pale for Tara to see any change in color of the Riprap man's "skin," she still thought he blanched at the image she'd shown him.

"How could you…You haven't the power to do that!" the Riprap man sputtered. Then he narrowed his eyes at her. "Or the will."

Tara had to acknowledge that. "As I said, I don't want to utterly destroy you. That doesn't mean I won't. You need to forsake your vengeance on me. You've already outlived your original purpose. Portland is safe from the river spirit. Go and live in the mountains, where your true heart lies."

"No," the Riprap man said, shaking his head hard. "I will hunt you to the end of your days. Then I will kill your black lover and all your friends."

Tara cocked her head to the side. She was surprised that he wasn't threatening the coven specifically. Or had he not realized that she'd formed one? They had met at Hallowed Ground, a place protected by Kaede. And ze was good with spaces.

"You can try," Tara said. "But first you have to catch me."

Tara made as though to leap back onto another boulder, further down the bank.

She was surprised by how fast the Riprap man could move, flying back off the boulder he was standing on and landing on the bank beside her.

"No. The time for your arguments and pretty words has come to an end. Now, you must die," the Riprap man said.

This time, instead of trying to wrap his arms around her and throw her into the water, he wrapped his hands around her neck. Lifting her completely off the ground, he started to choke her.

Tara struggled. She bruised her hands beating at the solid rock arms holding her. She kicked out, contacting his torso with a thud, sending sharp pain through her foot but his grip didn't falter.

With a gasp, Tara pulled in as much air as she could. She knew she didn't have much time before this soul body blacked out. Her throat hurt and she couldn't breathe. Dark spots started to form in front of her eyes.

Tara reached deep inside of herself and grabbed the fire always banked there. She sacrificed a little of her precious air to bring it to a flame.

The Riprap man let Tara fall back to the ground. Through watering eyes, Tara watched the Riprap man beat out the tiny fires that had started on his bowler, scorching his head.

With a growl of disgust, the Riprap man finally knocked the hat to the side. The mud abruptly put out the flames.

"That was my best hat," he complained, turning his focus back to her. "Now, you must die."

He grabbed her neck again, holding it in a crushing embrace. She felt him prying at her as he stole her air. He was intent on sucking every bit of magic from her, as he'd stolen Soot. He would take the fire, the earth, and finally, her water abilities.

No, Tara said. She couldn't speak aloud, but she could deny his attack with every fiber.

She felt his hooks traveling inside her, along the quicksilver core of her being. She flayed them with fire whenever they landed, melting them to regain the power.

There were too many of them, all diving deep inside of her, trying to trawl out all of her magic.

Tara turned her focus outward again. *No*, she said again, denying him. *You are the one starting to come apart.*

She stared at his chest, that misshapen pile of rocks.

With as much force as she could call up, she *pushed* at him, pushed at that weak spot, trying to get him to topple apart.

A massive shudder went through the Riprap man. His grip on her neck weakened and she took a gasping, shuddering breath.

"What are you doing?" he demanded, shaking her.

It was almost worse than being choked. All her limbs flew away as he shook, bruising her body further. She felt like a ragdoll in the mouth of a terrier shaking with all his might.

"I am *not* a killer," Tara croaked. "I will not merely slaughter you." She focused her power for one last push, sparking as she went, shoving against the creases of his chest.

The Riprap man dropped Tara on the ground. Her knees buckled under her and she landed on all fours. She gasped again, drawing more air in, though it felt like she was swallowing glass.

"I'm not destroying you," Tara said again. "I'm stripping you of your power."

The Riprap man turned huge, horrified eyes at her. "You—you can't!" he said. "You're just a witch!"

Slowly, Tara pushed herself up to standing. She swayed as though mighty winds whirled around her.

"You're right. I am just a sole witch. One with a powerful coven backing her," she said. She pointed her finger at him, directing all the power she felt swirling around the area. "Tell me. What will Mulinohana do when he realizes that you've forsaken him?"

Tara raised her other hand, then made a rending

motion, tearing an imaginary veil apart. "Your bond is broken," she said, her words taking on a chanting quality. "I release Mulinohana. The river spirit is now free to choose its own companion."

"NO!!!" shouted the Riprap man. He made grabbing motions with his hands, as if trying to trap the pieces of himself that were flying away.

The river roared in response, an angry tide set on washing away everything in its path. Out of the corner of her eye, Tara could see the water leaping high, though it stayed within its banks.

"I free the water spirit Mulinohana from your bond," Tara shouted over the sound of the rushing water. "In this place where the bond was first formed. The water is free as it always should be, to find its own way. I release Mulinohana from the ties that bind you together. The water no longer has to accept your rock boundaries. Be free!"

The power of the coven swirled up around Tara. Instead of a golden net of healing, it was a dark cloud, sparking with fire, gibbering to itself as it descended on the Riprap man.

Groans of breaking rock overwhelmed the sound of the running water. The Riprap man shrieked again, as if his soul was being torn apart.

Tara made herself stay and listen. She was the one who wrought this. She needed to bear the consequences of her decisions.

The dark cloud rose up finally, streaks of blue now dancing through it. It flew out over the water, dissipating into mist, sparkling bits of magic falling down into the calming waters.

In front of Tara, a solid man of rock still stood. Except he'd shrunk in all his proportions, and now stood a head shorter than Tara instead of towering over her. His torso still showed signs of their battle, and creaked when the Riprap man took a small step forward.

It was his eyes, however, that showed what he'd lost. Tara would say that he had the look of a damned soul, with nothing but Hell before him.

"What have you done?" he croaked, his smooth voice gone.

"I've broken the bond between you and Mulinohana," she said. "Or rather, we have." She still felt a thread of magic tugging her back to where her physical body still sat. "The river spirit can now choose a more appropriate companion. I suspect it only chose you because you were there. Not because you were the best suited."

The Riprap man shook his head. "No. You are wrong. I sacrificed the others who might have taken my place. Mulinohana chose me because I was strongest."

"And came to regret that choice," Tara reminded him. "The river spirit longs for someone who is more aligned with him."

"No!" the Riprap man screamed. Though his voice had grown stronger, he still looked frail, as if the first strong wind might send the haphazardly balanced rocks of his body toppling. "You are wrong. And you are the one who will live to regret your choice."

"Do you really want to fight me again?" Tara

threatened. She truly didn't want to destroy this creature, to wield that dark knife of power.

She would, though, if she had to.

"I won't be coming for you the next time," the Riprap man warned. "Mulinohana will. And I will give you no aid."

With that, the Riprap man disappeared.

Tara blinked, surprised. What did he mean that the river spirit was coming for her? The headwaters behind her still rushed, but they seemed much calmer, now. She couldn't sense any presence or malice.

After taking another painful breath, Tara sang a quiet hymn to the waters, fresh born and mighty, carrying their life-giving essence down from the purity of the mountains to the vastness of the oceans.

A cold wind blew across her hand. Tara looked down to find Soot sitting beside her. He looked happy to see her, eager to do her bidding.

Tara held the image of rose petals firmly in her mind, then of her scattering them across the water.

Soot disappeared in an instant, reappearing two breaths later. Only he wasn't in a solid dog form. Instead, he appeared to be made of petals himself, the red and pink forming the outline of a dog.

Tara directed him out over the water, blowing himself along, downstream, dropping petals as he went. Then she sang another short hymn of praise to the waters.

She had the sense that they were pleased with her action when she stepped back. The gray clouds peeled back from the sky, revealing the cool blue of autumn.

The threads linking Tara's soul to her body tugged on her again. She closed her eyes for a moment, giving thanks, promised to honor the waters again at the solstice as well as the equinox before she looked around one last time.

The waters appeared calm. She still didn't sense any malice in them.

Yet, there was an awareness in the river that hadn't been there before.

Would the river spirit really come after her? She doubted it. It should be grateful to no longer be bound to the Riprap man.

Bowing her head one last time, Tara followed the magical thread back to where her body awaited her.

TARA STUBBORNLY SAT OUT ON THE BALCONY OF THE porch, dressed in a sweater, jeans, leggings, and wrapped in a blanket. It wasn't really raining, just misting, hard. Tara welcomed the gray clouds, the turning of the season, from the overly hot summer to fall. She had what she thought of as an autumn tea, with chrysanthemum, rose, and borage petals, along with some lemon balm and apple mint.

Soot sat beside her. It had been easy to rebind him now that the influence of the Riprap man had faded, the words falling from her lips effortlessly. It would take a powerful coven to rend them apart.

She was aware that she belonged to him as much as he belonged to her. They needed one another. Some of the wind's carefree nature had been replaced with obedience to her. In return, Tara knew that she'd never breathe easy again without him near.

Kaede had suggested a *gotoku neko* for a fire familiar—a tri-colored Japanese hearth cat, with a short stubby tail. In folklore, it blew on a bamboo tube to coax flames from the coals.

Tara wasn't ready for another creature in her life. Not yet. Soot was going to be more than enough for the time being. Plus, once she bound a fire element, that would mean that she had officially passed further within, to the next circle, the circle of fire.

She needed time to just be.

Tara took another sip of her tea, looking out on the gray, soggy world. Tomorrow, she'd begin the process of moving to her new place. The room she was renting was only about the size of Kyle's guest room, so she wasn't upgrading there. And she was going to be sharing a house with three other people.

But it was house with a backyard and a garden, as well as a porch that she could just see the Willamette from. When she looked at a map, she realized that her life was now a triangle, with the three corners being Hallowed Ground, the Y, and her new home.

It felt right to her. Balanced.

She still wasn't sure what the Riprap man had meant that the river spirit would be coming after her. She'd gone to walk next to the river many times and it hadn't reached out to her or tried to coax her under the water. If anything, it felt more indifferent to her. She still sang to it on her morning walks, hymns of praise, and she scattered rose petals as well, brought to her by Soot.

Tara had thought that after her first battle with the Riprap man that she was ready to move forward. She'd been wrong. She'd needed to rest first, recover, accept her power and her position.

As well as build her team.

How long would it all last? Out of habit, Tara felt herself still holding her breath, metaphorically speaking, as if there would be another shoe dropping soon.

And there might be.

In the meanwhile, she was finally ready, and comfortable, with who she was and where she was going.

It was about time to stretch those wings of hers and fly.

EPILOGUE

Those interfering witches had no idea *the trouble they have wrought. By releasing the river spirit, they have doomed the city. They can talk of man's mighty works all they want. They have no idea what true power looks like, have never stood in the middle of flood waters rushing unheedingly toward their homes. They will learn. My time has not been wasted. The witches I sacrificed not only protected the bridges, they satisfied the river god, so that he wouldn't punish man. No more. When they come to me, begging for help, I will laugh and turn my back on them. The city has never known the name of her protector. But she will learn the name of her destroyer. Tara.*

Wilson Evermore, the Riprap Man, Unbound, 2019

READ MORE!

Be sure to read all the books in this completed series!

Circle of Air
Circle of Fire
Circle of Water
Circle of Earth

Available at your favorite retailers!

ABOUT KNOTTED ROAD PRESS

Knotted Road Press publishes dynamic fiction set in exotic locations and unique non-fiction voices in genres such as autobiography, business, cookbooks, and how-to. Our authors cover a wide range of genres including science fiction, fantasy, mystery, literary, and poetry, appealing to all readers. We offer both DRM-free ebooks and print books for a global readership.

Knotted Road Press
www.KnottedRoadPress.com
www.KnottedRoadPress.com/Shop

www.ingramcontent.com/pod-product-compliance
Lightning Source LLC
Chambersburg PA
CBHW070653100726
47907CB00007B/2190